THE SOFT EXILE

The Soft Exile

ERIC KIEFER

Pancake Massacre Publishing

For Mongolia. Thank you, and I'm sorry.

$$\sim\ 1\ \sim$$

PART ONE

<u>The Dunghill Raconteur and the Suicide Pact</u>

When I first agreed to volunteer for the United States Peace Corps, four stagnant years out of college and desperate as dying to prove that I was one of the Good People, I thought that I was going to save the universe.

I was going to walk through an airport archway and become a saint-in-residence... ease the hunger of the bowl-bellied, fly-eyed children... dig irrigation canals with my bare hands... heal lepers with my mind... compensate for the foul and demented cruelties of modern times... justify my existence... earn heaven... Eric the Redeemer... Eric the Guardian... all of that glorious savior stuff.

But in later times, whenever I would talk about the *real* reason that I volunteered to spend two years of my life living in a tent on the outskirts of the Gobi Desert, the conversation would always start with the same question:

"So what made you decide to join the Peace Corps, any-way?"

And my answer would always be the same... "It was either join the Corps or blow my fucking brains out."

***

All in all, there was really no reason why I should've wanted to kill myself.

Yes... I'm THAT guy... the one with the normal childhood in suburban New Jersey... the one with two loving parents and a sensitive shitload of siblings and relatives... the one who grew up with all his limbs and motor functions and mental conditioning in place... the one who was told to "Eat Your Vegetables!" because there were starving people in China... the one with a five-year university degree... the one with enough pocket money to have a weekly tab at the bar... the one who was taught to appreciate Hemingway and Kafka and Orwell and Kerouac... the one with a healthy appetite and a sincere smile... the one with a blind lust for Justice and a normal-sized penis.

So all in all, there was really no reason why I should've held that .38 revolver to my head.

And that's *exactly* what I told the suicide hotline worker.

***

She wasn't impressed, as it turned out.

"So you put a gun to your head... Biiiiiiiigggg Deeeeeal-llllll," the hotline worker told me that terrible Sunday afternoon, a forced kindness tempering her vowels. "Tell me something that I haven't heard before."

"You're really good at your job, you know that?" I said, trying to keep the bitterness from seeping into my voice. "Your compassion knows no bounds."

"Everyone on staff completes a mandatory three hours of compassion training," my telephone savior retorted. "But look, let's get back to the subject at hand. The HOW is irrelevant with a suicide attempt... what we're after is the WHY. So exactly what's the problem, here? You've got a roof over your head, food on your table, all your limbs and digits and organs, a college degree, a loving family, and two steaks a week for dinner. I mean, holy hell, you're living the American Dream! What terrible injustice could make you want to do something as crazy as killing yourself?"

"If I tell you, you'll just laugh," I mumbled.

"We're given strict instructions not to laugh," she assured me. "You've got my full attention."

After a wary pause, I told her, "I think it's because of Sausuage McMuffins."

"Sausuage McMuffins?"

"I don't know. It's... it's hard to explain," I finally answered, more *ashamed* than embarrassed to admit the truth. "It's not just Sausage McMuffins, I guess. It's the million daily atrocities of modern America. It's hotdog eating contests and strip malls and prime-time television. It's one-minute Ramen noodles, and one-hour photo shops and the Home Shopping Network all day long. It's the way we publicly finance billion-dollar sports stadiums, while homeless people die from malnutrition a block away. It's... It's all too big. The whole thing is just too goddamn big. And nobody can do anything about it."

Suddenly, the phone was as heavy as lead in my hand.

"Do you want to know the last thing that I saw this morning, right before I decided to put that gun to my head?" I asked. "It was a Sausage McMuffin. That's right... a goddamn Sausage McMuffin. That's what set this whole thing off. See, I had gone out to the goddamn fast food place, come back with breakfast, and was about to sit down and take a bite from my sandwich, when for whatever reason, I took a closer look at my food. Now, I've been eating McDonalds since I was five – about ten years longer than I've been smoking – and there's nothing about a Sausage McMuffin that I haven't seen before. But this morning I must have had a new pair of eyes, because I suddenly wasn't seeing a breakfast sandwich in front of me. It was something much different... and I'm not sure that I can truly explain what I saw, even now."

"Try me," she challenged.

"The big picture," I said. "I saw the big picture."

The hotline worker was silent then, and I thought for a moment that she might have hung up. But after a minute she cleared her throat and told me to go on.

"A Sausage McMuffin is not a simple thing," I continued. "It is the Zeitgeist of the twentieth century, and most likely, of the twenty-first century as well. Just think about it. For every Sausage McMuffin that is lifted to some bastard's mouth, there is a cycle of death and misery and exploitation that sums up modern America better than any poet, author, musician, artist or mystic has ever managed.

"The meat for a McDonalds breakfast sandwich, for example, comes from an industrialized factory farm, where the cattle are dotted with bleeding ulcers and pumped full of antibiotics to keep them from dropping dead where they stand. Once this meat is harvested, processed and flash frozen, it is loaded onto a refrigerated trailer and hauled hundreds of miles to its eventual destination... the local McDonalds. It is here that the employee-slaves of the ruthless McDonalds corporation assemble the ingredients for a Sausage McMuffin, working fifty hours a week for minimum wage. Here, they serve those sandwiches to a bleary-eyed horde of equally exhausted worker bees that have arrived for the daily feed. And all the while, the Sausage McMuffin grows stronger, more powerful. All the while, the beast is fed."

I paused to catch my breath before continuing. "As I gazed down at that lousy sandwich this morning, I suddenly realized that everyone, even myself, shares responsibility for every last bit of all that weird terror and madness... and not just at McDonalds, but in the totality of our lives, as well. As I sat there looking at my sad, little breakfast, I realized that the whole world was right in front of me... the whole universe... right in one, greasy breakfast sandwich. And do you know what? I'm part of it all... that's the sick joke. That's what made me finally crack. I'm just as guilty as everyone else. Because, God help me, the goddamn things are delicious! Delicious!"

"And that's when you first got the idea to put a gun to your head?" my hotline worker asked.

I slowed down for a moment, running my hand through my hair, listening to the faint static of the phone line fiber optics. "Yeah, well, I mean... what chance do we have to be Good People, when everything we do, everything we consume, everything we are, is part of the problem? It's all too big... and not even Ghandi or MLK managed to stop it. You can't stop the million Sausage McMuffins of modern existence... you just can't. Ask old Joe Hill if he saved the world. Ask Cesar Chavez, or Einstein, or any of those other countless saints. You can fight your entire life, maybe change an entire generation, but the Bastards will always be camped right there on the sidelines, waiting for you to let your guard down, waiting for the Red Sea to part again so they can swarm on through and stomp your ass to Kingdom Come. And the thing is, we know that there isn't a goddamn thing that we can do about any of it. Sure, we can cut a check for the latest, hippest pledge drive. We can populate the protests, or trade in our SUVs, or write letters to some asshole in Congress. But deep down, even the most gullible of us has got to know that these puny efforts don't really change a single thing. History whips around like a boomerang snake, repeating itself endlessly, just with better technology. There will always be hatred, and there will always be obedience. We devour ourselves. There's no hope. What's the value of one Good Person in a world like this? Hell, what's the value of one good deed?"

For a while, the hotline worker remained quiet. When she spoke again, her voice was transformed, purged of its earlier vitriol and sarcasm.

"What is the value of a good deed?" she asked. "Do you honestly want to know what I think? No bullshit... no fake compassion... raw?"

"Yes," I said, after thinking it over for a moment. "I do."

She paused with a professional sadness, like a hangman about to reveal a secret to the condemned. "I think that your life depends on finding out."

We left it like that for a moment, each weighing our next words carefully.

It was she who spoke first. "You want to know the value of a good deed, huh? Well... OK. I hereby issue you a challenge. I'm giving you two years – that's twenty-four months – to find the answer to that question. If you haven't found one by then, I personally give you permission... on all of my vested authority as an official suicide hotline worker... to kill yourself in any gruesome way you deem fit."

"Really?" I asked.

"Really," she said.

I thought her offer over. Two years to take a last shot at redemption... two years of water coolers and traffic jams and subway stabbings and the Republican National Convention... two years alone in America, on the edge of a razor... two more years doomed to wander through The Cauldron... alive... without an exit.

"I don't know if I can make it that long," I admitted at last.

My suicide hotline worker coughed into the phone. "Well, there *is* something that I rarely recommend to any of my callers... kind of a last ditch, 'grand-gesture' type of thing... but in your case, I think that it might be worth looking into.

However, it's a secret that I'm not willing to give away for free. In exchange for this information, I want a promise. If you swear to give me two years, I mean really *promise*, then we've got a deal. But I want your word. Two years of life. And an answer to The Question. Do we have a deal?"

And just like that, I found myself saying, "OK. Two years. An answer to The Question. It's a deal. Now please... please... I need to know... what's this big idea of yours?"

My hotline worker laughed strangely, like a pimp whose customer has unknowingly chosen a hermaphrodite hooker.

"What do you know about the United States Peace Corps?" she asked.

And that's how it all began.

~ 2 ~

The Enlisted Man

For good or ill, scarce is the American who hasn't heard of the PEACE CORPS... that archetype among international aid organizations, the crème de la crème of the volunteering world, the gold standard of American humanitarianism. The mythology of the Peace Corps has permanently infused itself into our popular culture; its name is instantly familiar to even the most jaded of hedonists. It is - without a doubt - the sexiest kudos in all of American do-gooder society.

But if you need a reminder, here's their deal:

A brainchild of the JFK administration, the Peace Corps has been one of the American government's premier humanitarian aid programs for over forty years. A branch of the State Department – not the military, as many believe - the Peace Corps has three, simple missions:

Provide developing nations with trained and skilled volunteers... Educate foreign cultures about America... Educate Americans about foreign cultures.

To accomplish these missions, the Corps operates on a theory of "total cultural immersion", the idea being that the only way to truly understand the needs of an impoverished community is to *live* in one. For a Corps volunteer, this means two years of residing and working in a third-world community, during which he or she is often the only American for hundreds of miles in any direction. It's a combination of working in a soup kitchen and climbing Annapurna... real Mother Theresa-in-jeans-type shit.

Peace Corps volunteers have built wells, constructed computer labs, taught in schools, started co-ops, built domestic abuse shelters, worked in orphanages, built computer labs, trained farmers in sustainable agriculture, spearheaded A.I.D.S. awareness programs, organized disaster relief, cured cancer and walked on the moon. Past alumni include politicians, writers, diplomats, doctors, educators and captains of industry.

But as might be expected, it hasn't *always* gone well.

The Corps' early history is littered with instances of volunteers disappearing, dying or simply going psycho... some as the result of documented foul play, and many others under suspicious circumstances. Ironically, most of the violence that Peace Corps workers have suffered has been at the hands of their fellow volunteers, such as the infamous Tonga tragedy in the late 1970s, when a love-struck American lost his mind and stabbed a fellow volunteer to death.

But in the past few decades, the organization's safety policies have been thoroughly revamped and renovated, and the number of volunteer flip-outs has since been dwarfed by the sheer abundance of success stories. And in the end, the

Peace Corps is just the kind of thing that might save your soul... or so a little bird told me.

So I got an application and told a few lies.

And lo and behold, the bastards bought it.

***

When the Peace Corps recruiter called me on the phone for our initial interview, I told him about my plans to heal lepers and save the world. I asked him for something drastic and heroic. I asked him for something that would save my soul.

"That's not really how it's done anymore," he told me.

When he said that I would most likely be assigned a job as an English as a Second Language teacher, I nearly quit on the spot. But the recruiter promised me - off the record - that this was only an official reason to be in the country, my foot in the door so to speak, and eventually he wore me down.

"Lots of English teachers go on to make themselves useful," he assured me. "You want to heal lepers on the side, that's your business."

It was then that my recruiter offered me a spot in Mongolia, a landlocked country of three million people in Central Asia - the least-peopled place on the planet - an ancient nation of seasonal nomads and desert dwellers, of warriors and legends, brutal winters, herders, sandstorms, horses and shamanistic Buddhism.

Mongolia... the homeland of Ghengis-Fucking-Khan... the last earthly refuge of the true nomad... the land of the Endless Sky... the reason that the Great Wall of China exists.

MONGOLIA.

"Jeezus," I told him. "Don't you have anything available in Fiji or some goddamn place?"

It turned out that they did not... all hands were needed on deck for the Corps' expansion into the land of the Blue Sky. The nation had reached out to the United States Peace Corps with a bizarrely fervent request. Having recently freed themselves from a century of brutal Soviet repression in the Democratic Revolution of 1990, Mongolians now faced the challenge of switching to a free-market economy... a battle that the struggling nation had clearly been losing. At the turn of the century, about a quarter of their population was subsiding on about $1 USD a day. The rest of the Mongolian people were crammed into a handful of grotesquely swelling cities across the country, many of them living in near-slum conditions, while their "elected" representatives grew fat off the foreign developers and international mining companies who had come to pillage Mongolia during its time of transition.

As part of their mad rush to convert to a democratic, capitalist society, Mongolian political leaders reached out to the United States Peace Corps, asking the fabled agency to send them English teachers... hundreds of English teachers... all the English teachers they had... to help the country convert their national "Second Language" to American.

"We cannot succeed in a globalized world without our people knowing English," they pleaded. "Please send teachers. We implore you."

"We'll see what we can do," Peace Corps leaders told them.

And so that's how, three months later, I found myself in a dismal LAX hotel complex on a smoggy June morning, yanking my luggage through the air conditioned doorway of the Renaissance Hotel... a reluctant martyr on a soft exile... destined for Mongolia, or suicide, or Hell... whichever came first.

***

At first the hotel desk clerk gave me some hassle because I was a few hours early for check-in, but I must have looked pretty disgusting, having spent the previous night sleepless in a crappy L.A. hostel, and she eventually let me in when I told her that I was here to join the Peace Corps and save the world.

"Good luck with that," the clerk told me, handing me a room key.

"With what?" I asked.

"Saving the world," she said, the same way a person speaks about their New Year's resolutions. "Good luck with that, I mean. You know, sometimes I think about leaving all this behind, just like you're doing... going on some great adventure... maybe join the circus or something, I dunno."

"Sounds noble enough to me," I said, and turned to grab my gear.

"Do you need someone to help you with your bags?" the clerk asked.

"It's probably better if I take it myself," I said, thinking about the two joints of high-grade Sour Diesel that were stashed in my sweatsocks.

Waving goodbye, I drug my luggage up to the third floor, where the Corps had booked rooms for the 58 members of that year's envoy to Mongolia... the largest trainee group the country had ever seen. To save money, we had been doubled up in the hotel rooms. I walked up to room 3116 and flung the door open, immensely pleased to find nobody there yet. Throwing my stuff down on the bed by the window - the perpetual window seat taker - I looked out on the ghastly view... concrete balconies of the hotel next door with their lousy flowerpots and tan drapes.

With a constipated grimace, I decided to shut the blinds.

The Corps had scheduled an evening-long orientation session starting at three 'o' clock, so I took a shower, smoked a joint and made myself some hotel room coffee, then headed down to the lobby to watch America drift by, all the while half-hoping that some anonymous arm would reach out... grab me... and yank me back into The Cauldron before it was too late.

But not a single one did.

***

In the end, the "brief" Corps orientation session had lasted until seven that night. After the goddamn thing was finally over, I went down to the hotel bar to be alone.

As I slurped at my booze, I kept glancing uneasily over my shoulder. I've always had some inexplicable fear of getting drunk alone in Los Angeles. And at this point I trusted no one - this grey oasis was no place to make any sort of rational judgment of character. At a time like this, all a sane person can do is to make broad social observations from behind the safety of a pint glass.

At a time like this, all a man can do is hope.

I had gotten a chance to meet most of the other M-17 volunteers at orientation, and I wasn't impressed. We came from suburbs with bored police and old money: Auburn, Cheshire, Chandler, Rutherford, Skokie, Decatur and Kalamazoo. We came with college degrees and university debts. We came with ipods, and Rimbaud, and the indefatigability of impending martyrdom. We came with the communal conviction that we were an immense juggernaut, an irresistible force that was going to sweep across Mongolia - for whatever noble or self-satisfying purpose - because we were the shapers of the Earth and had the power to save or destroy the world.

Ha.

The Peace Corps is infamously meticulous in who they accept into their sacred tradition. College degrees, work and personal references, criminal background checks, health examinations... these are all bullwhips in a bureaucratic gauntlet which fifty percent of Peace Corps applicants never pass. The Corps struggles valiantly to strain out the flakes and the deserters, the thrill seekers and the cowboys, the felons and the liars, the weak-stomached and the infirm, the posers and the perverts, and above all, the hopelessly lost.

But if I had found my way in, there were bound to be others.

There is a psychological profile that the Corps has developed for their ideal Corps volunteer, the product of decades of coldly-clinical observation of their own trainees. This profile involves buzz words like "adaptable", "independent", "patient", "resourceful" and "motivated."

It also involves words like "compassionate", although to a much lesser degree.

***

To get its rookies ready for field duty, the Peace Corps puts each potential volunteer through a three-month, in-country hazing called "Pre-Service Training." This training period – PST in Corps' parlance - consists of three phases, which begin the day after orientation.

From the LAX airport, the new trainees fly to Ulaanbaatar – the Mongolian capitol – for Phase One of their training... the "Welcome to Mongolia" segment. Here, the rookies are fed enough emergency survival strategies to get them through the next few months with as few debilitating incidents as possible. They are also pumped full of immunizations and vaccines, and equipped with their official Peace Corps gear.

Typically, Phase One only lasts a few days. Its main function is as a staging point for Phase Two.

This phase – the "Home Stay" phase – takes place away from the comforts of the city, plunging the rookies into the lifestyle that the Corps has been promising all along... total cultural immersion. For three months, each trainee lives with an assigned "host family" in a rural Mongol village – much like a foreign exchange student – where they learn firsthand what it means to be Mongolian. During this time, the rookies are also subjected to grueling, daily training sessions that include intensive language and culture training, basic survival techniques, and job-specific technical training.

After the Home Stay phase, the now-salty Corps neophytes are taken back to Ulaanbaatar, where they are given their final assignments and shipped off to their numerous and scattered worksites across Mongolia. This final phase – the "Graduation" – is the culmination of PST. By this time, the rookies are expected to be able to conduct a basic conversation in Mongolian, start a fire from scratch, wash clothes by hand, chop and split their own wood, and teach an English class on the present progressive tense. Those who cannot are sent home to America.

And it's all downhill for those who remain.

***

After a few hours of vodka tonics at the hotel bar, I decided to go out to the patio and take in my last nighttime sky in America. The outdoor courtyard was empty, so I went and sat in a white, plastic patio chair, lit up a joint and stared up into the smoggy void that is the LAX skyline. The moon over the airport complex that night was like weak tea... a fat-clogged heart in its dying gasps. It was an utterly starless view, and it made me tired to look at it.

"Why aren't there any stars in this goddamn sky?" I muttered as I stretched out in the patio chair, not really sure what I would have done with stars at the moment anyway.

I was a background character in the Great Painter's over-burdened panorama, ready to walk off the frame and not be missed... art abandoning the artist. The spectral promise of Mongolia was so effortlessly slurping up the last remaining bits of American Guilt within me, and not only the dirty guiltiness of this L.A. airport hotel, but also of shopping malls, late night infomercials and automated car washes - the entire spectrum of false prophet materialism that screamed my name with every step - the endless ocean of deputized pimps and whores who controlled it - the whole dreary mess of modern America... and to shit with the stars, anyway.

As I sat there in my patio chair, a 747 passenger jet cut across the sky, and I followed its blinking lights until the plane disappeared over the horizon.

There but for the grace of Pan Am, go I.

Suddenly overcome with a fiendish desperation, overcome by a manic desire for purity, I stood up from my chair and threw my hands in the air, inspired to call out to the heavens and proclaim my faith in things to come. I wanted to believe in good again, even if it killed me. I wanted to holler out to a cruel universe that it was the Good Peoples' turns to shine, and that for once - for goddamn once! - we'd triumph over the forces of ignorance and death and apathy. I wanted to yell that there *was* such a thing as redemption, and it was on its way. I wanted to assure the world that I was still in love with it, after all.

But what actually came out of my mouth was "SO LONG, ASSHOLES!"... which I brayed out like I had Tourette's Syndrome... bawled forward into the sleepy, grey beyond of new-millennium America... surrendered in hostility to the hundred, anonymous, smog-stained windows of the Renaissance Hotel complex. "SO LONG... AND GOOD RIDDANCE!"

Lights began to flicker on in a few nearby hotel windows, so I took one last drag off my joint, flicked the roach into the pool and went back inside to my room, where I flipped the big hotel TV on to the Tonight Show and let Jay Leno's crummy voice wean me into a restless slumber.

And that was my last night in America.

~ 3 ~

Welcome to the Trenches!

It takes a lot of ugly language to get a group of 58 people on the same international flight.

Almost all of it comes during baggage check-in.

The Corps allots each new volunteer 102 total pounds of luggage, an amount that is quickly filled with socks and toothpaste, leaving little room for indulgences. The few personal belongings that a Peace Corps volunteer chooses to bring with them tell stories, reveal skeletons and uncover addictions. We had spent days cramming our lives into suitcases, and in most cases, we found that our lives simply couldn't fit. And now here we were, bare in the LAX baggage terminal, our souls on display in the baggage check-in lane, a people watcher's all-you-can-eat buffet.

Laptops loaded with compressed movies and secret pornography. Thesauruses. Bibles. Harmonicas. A student chemistry set. An industrial-strength hairdryer. A prosthetic leg. A solar powered backpack.

I had about ninety pounds of baggage with me: a Gibson six-string acoustic guitar, a few choice books, two week's worth of socks, boxers and t-shirts, two sets of thermals, two sweaters and pairs of jeans, a surplus U.S. Postal Service winter coat, a Salvation Army-rescued business suit and pants, two cartons of Camel Lights, a cheap mp3 player, a cheaper digital camera, some assorted "American" souvenirs to give out as presents, and a few other necessities such as a pocket flashlight and a good folding knife.

I'd gotten used to traveling light - my last move before I joined the Corps was done in a single trip in a Dodge Shadow hatchback – but the luggage limit weighed heavily on some of the other volunteers. For example, take poor little Eliza Lin and her humongous suitcase... at least ten pounds bigger than she was and easily thrice as wide. Now her luggage was fifteen pounds too heavy, the baggage clerk was tired of making exceptions, and Eliza was having a heart attack trying to find items to jettison.

Without being asked, I invited myself over for a closer look. I saw that Eliza had insisted on packing three pairs of heavy-duty latex dishwashing gloves, because as she later told me, she didn't want her hands to get "wrinkly."

"You probably don't need those," I told her, pointing at the gloves, trying to be helpful.

"You should always be prepared," she replied, fuming over her luggage and giving me a glare like I was a fool for not packing any.

***

After our détente at the baggage station, it took nearly 24 hours of flight time – and a layover in Korea - before we arrived in Mongolia.

I spent most of my down time reading my Lonely Planet travel guide, until twenty hours into the journey, I began to finally feel like I was really getting the hang of things. On our connecting flight from Korea, eager to put my knowledge to the test, I attempted to ask our pretty Mongolian flight attendant if I could have a cup of water in her native language.

The broad-hipped beauty smiled, and politely informed me in fluent English that I was asking for a plate of hair.

"I'll guess I'll take a Coke then," I told her, nodding.

As we drew close to Mongolia's borders, murmurs started to snake through the plane. I leaned my head against the window and cast my eyes downward. A soft layer of cumulous clouds framed the view from the airplane window, revealing a tremendous, open sky... so blue that it strained my eyes to look at it. Underneath it all, the rolling, emerald hills of summertime Mongolia seemed to expand forever, occasionally humping up into spectacular mountain ridges that ran for hundreds of miles. I was especially taken by the sparse roads - thin brown streaks among the green - which never seemed to cross each other, and blended imperceptibly with the local rivers and waterways. It was a sight to make Frank Lloyd Wright proud. In fact, every man-made structure that I could see seemed to be woven into the landscape... an entire horizon of uninterrupted, pastoral existence.

The Mongolian skyline was incalculable, even beyond what the fables had promised. And it was *blue*... the blue of dreams... the blue of sadness... the blue of immortality... an amazing blue whole-note, steady and permanent as a heartbeat. I had seen scenes like this in America before: Yellowstone, the Smoky Mountains, the Grand Tetons, Glacier National. But somehow, Mongolia seemed so much larger... so much older... so much deeper.

And goddamn, was it blue.

From that airliner, it was all beautiful. And despite my initial misgivings, I began to think that spending two years in Mongolia might not be that bad, after all.

Imagine, I thought. *Me... who has seen almost three decades worth of New Jersey asphalt... in Mongolia...with its thousand-year patience and infinite skies. And no shopping mall within a thousand miles...*

And I leaned back in my seat and laughed.

***

We arrived in Ulaanbaatar – the Mongol capital city – at 8:37 a.m. on June 3.

After touchdown at the Chingiis Khan International Airport, we were shuttled via charter bus to the Temujiin Tourist Camp, an "authentic" Mongolian living experience just outside Ulaanbaatar. Here, we spent the next three days in Phase One of our Pre-Service Training.

It was in this place that my feet first slapped Mongolian soil.

One of the many "authentic" Mongol tourist camps that had emerged in the past decade, Camp Temujiin was set back in the Mongolian countryside like a golf resort, situated among a series of gently rolling hills, remote and rustic, in a beautiful, agrarian landscape reminiscent of the Elysian Fields. However, the camp's main claim to fame was not its picturesque setting, but its traditional, "*ger*-style" housing.

Known to the western world as "yurts", the iconic, circular, Mongol house-tents known as *gers* are some of the simplest, yet most intriguing dwellings in the world. About the size of a small, studio apartment, a ger is made of a circular latticework of wooden support slats, which form a basic, teepee-like skeleton. Two insulating, outer layers of sheep felt are overlaid on this skeleton, and the whole thing is then anchored down with a system of well-weathered ropes. The end result is something ancient... something primal and matronly... like living in a womb.

Or tourist trap, as the case may be.

Despite its magnificent gers and rustic setting, I would soon learn that Camp Temujiin was authentic Mongol living in the same way that Taco Bell was authentic Mexican food. With its freshly-laundered sheets, pay-bar and flush toilets, the camp was little more than a gimmicky hotel for expats and tourists. The new Mongol wave of entrepreneurs had recognized the capitalistic "value" that lay in exploiting their heritage, and one result was the proliferation of camps such as these, which catered almost exclusively to corporate and state clientele on the lookout for an "authentic cultural experience."

But there is cultural... and there is *Culture*... and I still had a long way to go before I knew the difference.

***

We met the Corps' training staff soon after settling into our gers.

Apart from the country director and his assistant, the entire in-country Corps staff was composed of Mongolian citizens... born and raised Mongol, each one. They were the first real Mongolians that I had the opportunity to observe - airports and Wikipedia aside - and I tried to study them as best I could.

Dark tan in complexion with broad faces and high cheeks, Mongols are generally taller and stockier than their Asian neighbors. Many of their faces, even businessmen and bureaucrats, are wrinkled from a lifetime of exposure to the unforgiving Mongolian weather and the hard-charging lifestyle of their homeland.

Each staff member spoke fluent English, with differing degrees of hipness. It was something that they were extremely proud of, and rightly so. But I was amused to notice that almost all of them had a distinct Mongol tone of voice. Their accents buried themselves deep... guttural, throat-clenching consonants... brassy, ballsy, shout-across-the-room strength (even from the women)... and above all, that unmistakable and reflexive "kkkkkhhhhhhhhhhhhh" sound, the one that sounded like clearing the throat after eating too much chocolate.

I had come expecting to see our hosts clad in *dels* (the long, flowing, Jedi-like traditional robes of the rural Mongolian), but in the recent years, urban Mongols – especially those living in Ulaanbaatar - had been conforming more and more to the Eurocentric mode of dress and beauty. Robes began to be phased out in favor of t-shirts and blue jeans. The professional men and women in the city began wearing suits. The women began to shave their armpits and wear lipstick. The men had long ago cut off their barbarian braids.

And there wasn't a single del-wearer among the entire Corps staff.

My favorite among the bunch was a greasy, old bastard known as Gansugkh. One of the Corps' professional drivers/handymen, Gansugkh was the first to instruct me how to bum a cigarette in Mongolian, and he always had a new curse word to teach me in exchange for a smoke.

He was one of the only Corps staff members I bothered to exchange email addresses with, and he was also the only one that I ever bothered to write. It was a simple exchange. Fourteen months after PST, long after I had graduated from training and gone out to my permanent worksite, I sent an email to Gansugkh, asking him if he had any advice for someone who might be on the verge of losing his mind.

The bastard wrote back a day later, with a one-word reply...

"Vodka."

***

After meeting our instructors, we spent the rest of the afternoon picking up our official Corps gear.

We were each issued a negative-twenty-degree-rated sleeping bag, an electric water distiller, a backup hand-operated water filter, a small fire extinguisher, a mosquito net, a Peace-Corps certified surge protector, a set of poly-plastic snowshoes, a carbon monoxide/smoke detector, a portable, electric space heater, a ten-gallon wash basin, some Mongol-English teaching materials and a heavy-duty Nalgene water bottle.

Many of these items would later make excellent bribe material at our sites.

Each of us was also issued a small, black plastic case about the size of a nuclear football... our Corps medical kits. Inside were a cornucopia of pills: pseudoephedrine, ibuprofen, Benedryl, amoxicillin, Immodium AD, Ciprofloxacin (for diarrhea), Tamiflu (for the dreaded bird flu), dioxycyclin (for marmot plague) and of course, some good old penicillin (for everything else). The medical kits also came with two rolls of gauze, throat lozenges, antibacterial and antifungal creams, medical scissors, medical tape, a set of sterile latex gloves, sterile plastic tweezers, sunscreen, emergency eye-wash, dental floss, thermometer strips, chapstick, mosquito repellant, adhesive bandages, oral rehydrators, a six-pack of condoms (lubricated *and* non-lubricated), and most curious of all, a plastic rape whistle.

When I got my medical kit, I tried to blow the rape whistle. It didn't work.

The Corps staffers promised that they'd get me another as soon as possible.

"It's best to be prepared," was all they said.

***

Later that afternoon, we were treated to our first, traditional Mongol meal... MEAT!!!

It is MEAT!!! which composes the bulk of the Mongol menu... whether it be lamb, goat, beef, or even the occasional horse or camel. In addition, almost every dish in the Mongolian cuisine has heaping amounts of animal fat in it, saturated fat being the nutritional staple that compensates for their lack of fresh vegetables. MEAT!!! provides a Mongolian with his or her vitamins, minerals and essential proteins. It is their main course. It is their culinary destiny.

As might be expected, there are almost no vegetarians in Mongolia... or at least not any happy ones.

We ate our first native dinner in the big, communal ger at the center of the camp. Our places that night were generously laden with unseasoned hunks of sheep and goat flesh, steamed meat dumplings, vinegar-soaked carrot coleslaw, jarred pickles, potato salad, and endless jars of hard candy. It being an official Mongol ceremony of sorts, each table was also outfitted with two half-liter bottles of the country's premium hard spirit... Chingiis Vodka.

"You know," said the volunteer to my right, a scruffy college grad from Pittsburgh. "My grandfather always said that you can judge the character of a nation by its alcohol."

"Sounds like a wise man," I responded with gusto, tearing the seal off a bottle of vodka with my teeth. "Here's to prejudice."

***

For the rest of our days at Camp Temujiin, we split our time between language lessons and "Emergency Cultural Training"... a twisted charm school designed to get us through our first few months in Mongolia. For seven hours a day, we sat in the big, common-room ger at the south end of camp, our trainers trying their best to teach us how to avoid the larger cultural faux pas that would get us mugged, beaten, or worse.

Mongolians are physically affectionate people, the Corps staff told us. *We like to show friendship and affection by touch, so don't be offended if a friendly stranger puts his hands on your shoulder, or a coworker grabs your ass. It's not meant to hurt you... unless it is*, they said.

And you'll definitely know when that's the case.

We were taught what to do if we stepped on someone's foot (offer an immediate apology and handshake), or spilled any sort of dairy product (dip your finger in the liquid and touch your forehead to make amends). We were coached not to whistle indoors or lay valuables on the ground. We were told that an extended middle finger in Mongolia means that things are "average", and has nothing to do with its insulting American cultural equivalent. We were trained to never hand someone a knife edge first, or step on the threshold of a ger. We were warned to never, ever play the "got your nose" game... whatever the reason... no matter how cute the child. We were instructed to always take at least one sip of vodka that has been offered in friendship, or at least pretend as if we did.

But above all, we were instructed to keep smiling... always smiling... because nobody likes a surly foreigner.

And indeed, as we neared the end of PST barely three months later, we were all reminded of what we'd learned in those first days in Camp Temujiin. On August 17, a Japanese foreign aid worker volunteering in Ulaanbaatar was discovered lying in his apartment bathtub... with his head bashed in and his apartment ransacked. According to the Mongolian press, the crime was described as "a burglary gone wrong."

JAPANESE TEACHER MURDERED IN U.B., the headline screamed.

Police made no arrests, although they were quoted as saying they were close to naming a suspect. The twenty five year-old, foreign-aid volunteer was in his second year of teaching Japanese at a city school, and there was no official word as to whether he was targeted specifically because he was a foreigner.

But *we* knew the truth.

He had stopped smiling.

***

After three days at Camp Temujiin, we prepared to ship out for Phase Two of our training... The Home Stay.

Since there was no single village that could absorb the enormous impact of four dozen raw Americans, the Corps divided us into seven groups, each of which was assigned to a different "host community" for the next three months. As per the Corps' plan, the groups would have little contact between each other during this time, forcing each pack of Americans to cooperate... or destroy themselves.

I ended up in a group headed for a small, riverside village called Delgerkhovd, a Podunk of 3,000 people in the central Selenge province, about a hundred kilometers out of the capitol city.

With me were six other volunteers:

Eddie was a straight-edged, big-bearded photo buff from Vermont. He had never had a drink of alcohol in his life, and his right eye had already begun to acquire a slight tic from squinting behind a camera so much. He was convinced that his photos would end up on the cover of National Geographic someday (his secret reason for being in Mongolia), and was constantly shooting every weird scene that he came across, proclaiming it to be "wicked."

Vinko, a tall Croatian from Chicago, was lost on some noble Hemmingway-esque adventure. Everything with Vinko had to be "authentic": toilets, food, weather, women. He'd end up - like me - requesting the most "hardcore" site assignment the Corps had available. He was a searcher, obsessed with living the nomadic life... an OK guy.

Abbie from Oregon was one of the new wave of humanitarian Grrl Power women, a skater chick as well as an ardent Buddhist. She was a little shy and skittish at first, and tended to disappear like a turtle inside her Against All Authority tour jacket in moments of stress. Shortly after we first met, I asked Abbie why she joined the Peace Corps. She replied that ever since she was a kid, she had this weird belief that if she suffered more, somehow the world would suffer less. "I mean, I know that suffering is the root of all existence," she said, "But there's got to be only so much of it to go around... don't you think?"

Ray was a handsome, six-foot son of a Georgia architecture professor, who all the Corps females had nicknamed "Hot Ass." Despite this nickname - which no woman was afraid to use to his face - he was a humble and intelligent guy, and you could tell that his new Peace Corps moniker really got on his nerves. He was constantly talking about his father - a former volunteer in Ghana - and you could tell that his old man was the main reason that Ray had come to Mongolia.

Ralph was a recent graduate of Brown University, a hulking brute of a bastard who told me that he wanted to work for Amnesty International one day. Ralph said that he joined the Peace Corps because it would be a good job reference, and he was dead serious. I could tell he was kind of grossed out by the Third World, because he walked around looking like he was motion sick all the time. The man drowned *everything* he ate in ketchup, the entire time he was in Mongolia.

Finally, there was redheaded **Bridget**, the firefly from Phoenix, Arizona. The thing that I liked best about Bridget was that she was honest about her apathy towards "saving the world." She had a penchant for getting stinking drunk and disappearing for long stretches of time, and had no problem with falling asleep in class. I could tell that Bridget had a good heart underneath it all, but it took me a long time to figure out just why the hell she was in the Corps in the first place... international vacations are expensive.

And so it was that a New England shutterbug, a Croatian adventurer, an Oregon skate-hippie, an Atlanta prettyboy, a Rhode Island Ivy-leaguer, an Arizona boozer and a suicidal writer from New Jersey became a temporary family... or at least made a half-assed attempt to.

The Delgerkhovd Seven.

***

Of course, the Corps had not sent us to Delgerkhovd alone. After all, that would be cruel, and they no longer did things that way.

Riding shotgun were our Peace Corps-hired "language and culture" teachers for the summer, a pair of Delgerkhovd natives named Oyunn and Chimgee. The two had been tasked not only with teaching us how to speak conversational Mongolian from scratch in ninety days, but also with babysitting us while we were in PST... *making sure that we don't do anything that get us lynched*, as Ralph later paraphrased.

I had gotten a chance to meet the pair at Camp Temujiin, shortly after the Peace Corps had divided us into training groups. Oyunn was the squatter of the two, with a broad face like one of those huge cookies that you get at the mall, and it seemed as if she was always in some sort of motion. Chimgee, with her elongated neck and slightly sad smile, looked a little like a melancholy crane. She had a perpetual droop to her eyes, as if she were stoned all day. The pair complemented each other well, with Oyunn doing most of the talking and Chimgee doing most of the observing.

They were excited to be returning home – the pair had been stuck in the city for two weeks now – and they promised us all that they would do their absolute best to help us "be safe."

The first time that we met, Oyunn told me that we would all be her "little cows."

"Excuse me?" I asked, not sure that I'd heard her right.

"Cows," Oyunn repeated, as Chimgee nodded in agreement. "You will be our cows."

Seeing that I still didn't understand, Oyunn explained that in Mongolia, the cow is considered one of the most resourceful and helpful creatures in the world. Its milk is a staple of the Mongolian diet, its labor enables farmers to feed their families, its dried dung is a highly efficient fuel for heating and cooking.

"In fact, there is an old Mongol fable about the cow," Oyunn told me. "It will help you understand what we mean..."

Long ago when the world was being made, the Creator was giving out kidneys to all the animals. The cow, who always takes her time to arrive anywhere, came upon the scene late, and there were no more kidneys left, only little scraps that none of the other animals wanted.

When the others animals saw what had happened, they became sad, and began to cry. "This will surely mean the end for cow," they mourned.

But the Creator told them not to worry. "Cow," he said. "I know who you are. Your milk nourishes the body, your dung fires the stove, your shoulders tug the plow and sow the fields. Mongolia has need of you... just as you have need of it."

The Creator then took all the spare bits and squeezed them between his hands, and when he unfolded them, there was a single, large kidney in its place. And that's why the cow has such a large kidney.

"Do you understand now?" Oyunn asked when she was done with her fable.

"Not really," I admitted.

"You are the cow," said Oyunn. "And it is our job to squeeze you a kidney."

***

So it was that the Delgerkhovd Seven (plus two) departed from Camp Temujiin on a bright June morning, destined for our new village and three months of cultural immersion training... happily crammed into a Corps-hired passenger van... the sun at our backs... our eyes glittering and our souls eager... seven ambassadors to the land beyond Bed Bath and Beyond.

Despite our eagerness, our journey to the village began slowly.

There are a few, semi-paved roads connecting the handful of large cities, but the majority of rural travel in Mongolia is done on pockmarked dirt roads, carved into the landscape by nothing more than sheer gumption and a decade worth of tire tracks. These pseudo-roads twist and wander with a maddening schizophrenia, often branching into several tributaries that rejoin a hundred kilometers down the line. They are hijacked by craters and road ravines, and in many spots they end abruptly and melt back into the steppe... ghost tracks on their way to nowhere. As a result of this, no driver will ever take the exact same path twice, or even *could* if they wanted to. The roads of Mongolia can be driven, yet they have no names. They exist and don't exist at the same time.

It is in this sense, that they are both blessed and damned.

My fellow volunteers seemed just as taken with the sheer nakedness of the Mongolian boulevard. "Is it true that Mongolia has less than 500 miles of paved road?" asked Abbie from the back seat.

"Yes, this is true," replied Oyunn.

"Amazing," marveled Eddie, leaning out the window so he could take a picture.

"Fucked-up," mumbled Ralph, edging out of Eddie's way.

There were no road signs, rest stops or jug handles on this primitive highway. No vending machines or fast food detours or even median lines. In fact, the whole journey reminded me of some weird, Gonzo-esque journey to the "Heart of the Mongolian Dream." There is an overwhelming grandeur to the initial Mongolian experience, one which often leaves first-time visitors feeling as if they've inadvertently strode right into the opening credits of the Magnificent Seven. It is a place where Time has hiccupped, and the old ways still apply. And as I gazed out on this beautiful world, straddling the edge of Forever, a primal urge prickled deep inside me.

Without realizing it, I began to belt out Dylan's "Highway 61 Revisited":

Now the rovin' gambler he was very bored
He was tryin' to create a next world war
He found a promoter who nearly fell off the floor
He said I never engaged in this kind of thing before
But yes I think it can be very easily done
We'll just put some bleachers out in the sun
And have it on Highway 61...

As I finished the last line of the stanza, our driver turned to me and asked something in Mongolian.

"What did he say?" I asked Oyunn.

"He asked what your song meant," she translated.

"Awww... nothing means anything in America," I told her, shrugging, but something must have been lost in the ensuing translation, because the driver just nodded at me pityingly like I was an idiot.

***

We arrived in Delgerkhovd around three 'o' clock, already ragged from our brief trip across the province.

At first, the view was fantastic.

The village was located on the banks of the Kharaa river, which snaked its way through town like smoke curling off a pipe. At the village's north border – extending for miles - was a gorgeous series of low-lying hills, and to the south, the village was bordered by a range of mountains, these much higher in altitude and ringed with crowns of clouds. Vast ranges of countryside lay to the east, and to the west lay the road to Ulaanbaatar, which wound like a dusty serpent back the way we'd come. In the center of it all lay Delgerkhovd itself... a tiny cluster of one-story concrete buildings, wooden shacks and old-fashioned ger tents... enfolded neatly within the valley like a well-constructed Hollywood prop.

It was all a beautiful sight... at first. But when our van finally pulled up within view of the village, there was no doubt that we had arrived – at last – in the Third World.

About half of the villagers still lived in ger tents, and the rest lived in Frankenstein-sloppy jumbles of spare 2x4s and rusty metal, complete with leaky tin roofs and rotting support beams. I could see at a glance that only about half of the homes were hooked up with electricity, and only a fraction of those had any sort of plumbing. A surprising amount of litter and rubbish festooned the area: candy wrappers, metal scraps, broken glass, discarded clothing, bottle caps and old batteries.

To my surprise, most of the villagers were wearing secondhand, western-style clothes: jeans, t-shirts, sweatpants and button-down Oxfords. It was as if the entire village had been outfitted by a Goodwill store. Here and there, giggling children roamed the streets in packs, and hundreds of wandering goats, chickens, sheep and cows sauntered through the village with impunity. Elder Mongols shuffled through the streets at a snail's pace, dressed in old, ratty robes that scraped the ground behind them, barely giving us a look as we passed. Tired-looking men leaned against rickety hashaa fences, smoking hand-rolled cigarettes and staring at our troupe of Americans with a blank curiosity.

"Jesus Christ," Ralph muttered, rolling up his window. "I feel like somebody's about to come by and offer to wash our windshield."

I shook my head, but secretly, I knew that he was right in a twisted way. Delgerkhovd was a different world from Camp Temujiin, where the only natives that we encountered were paid to smile at us and shake our hands. It was a dangerous place for the unwary – all of us could sense it right away – and there was no use denying that. All about me there was a curious, vast and incalculable vibration, as if I was seeing a world that hadn't changed for thousands of years... a universe that could swallow me up and assimilate me with no effort at all, like a Venus fly trap digesting a meal.

It was a world that was hungry, desperate and poor... but also content.

It was a world that had no idea I was coming... and didn't much care.

And for the first time since arriving in Mongolia, I began to think that saving the world might not be as easy as I thought.

~ 4 ~

Pre-Service Training

The three-month, Peace Corps training process is kind of like being a foreign exchange student... only the stakes are much higher, and there's not much chance of getting laid.

Pre-Service Training is a rookie volunteer's introduction to the *real* Mongolia. The target goal is total cultural assimilation. For three months, volunteers live with one of the Corps' carefully selected host families, who have all pledged to give their volunteer an "authentic" Mongol social experience... and not to spare the shit. As compensation for the immense inconvenience, each host family is reimbursed $140 USD per month, more than many of them usually make in half a year.

The host families are told that they should treat their volunteer as if he or she is one of the clan. "Treat them just like one of the family..." the Corps tells them. "Just like a Mongolian."

So for ninety days, each volunteer lives as a rural Mongol does. They bathe in the river. They partake in the family meals. They are forced to speak and hear Mongolian at all times. They squat in outhouses, eat sheep intestines, wake up with bedbugs and wash their clothes by hand.

They adapt.

They assimilate.

And as a result, one out of ten will not make it out of PST.

***

My own host family - the Dansarans - had hosted two volunteers before, one who later served for three years in the distant province of Khovd, and another who quit the Corps after two weeks. None of the family spoke English, apart from a few emergency phrases, such as "Call the police!" and "Do you need a doctor?"

I was told that they knew "what to expect" from an American.

Their home was architecturally-Spartan, a glorified shack with a tin roof and chapping paint. All around the house, frayed and amateurish electrical wiring jutted from random points in the walls, throwing off occasional - but terrifying - sparks. The only water in the house came from the village's public water pump, which the Dansarans stored in a big metal jerrycan in the mudroom. There was no plumbing, only a dry sink in the corner of the kitchen (with a plastic bucket underneath to catch the slop water), which needed to be emptied every day.

The place reminded me of something from one of Thoreau's wet dreams.

My host mother, Solongo -"Solo" as everyone called her - was the main gravitational force that kept the household in orbit. Her job as the village school's librarian was the only real family income, but Solo still managed to find the time to control almost every facet of what transpired under the Dansaran roof. She paid the bills. She cooked the meals. She signed the forms. She doled the punishments. And while the Confucian family order (supremacy of the father and first-born son) applied in name, there was no question who wore the *omd* in the Dansaran family.

After all, Mongolian families are not democracies; they are benevolent dictatorships.

I liked the three Dansaran siblings - Nyamdorj, Bymbadorj and Davasuren – as soon as I met them, although it took me almost two weeks before I realized that each of them had been named after a day of the week: Sunday, *Nyam*, Saturday, *Bymba*, and Monday, *Davaa.*

The eldest son, "Nyam" for short, was a good kid, six-foot tall, studiously-natured and proud of his responsibilities as the first-born male. He was quiet and reserved - almost subdued at times - and spent most of his time studying or working in the fields with his father. Overall, he treated me with a courteous deference - like an employee treats his boss when invited out to the bar for drinks.

The younger son, Bymba, was short and wiry, with a crafty but honest look perpetually plastered on his face. His hair was cut in a sharp but shaggy mop, and he had a number of freckles on his cheeks, unusual for a Mongolian. Like many of the new wave of Mongol youth, Bymba was fascinated by American hip hop culture, and was hugely disappointed when he found out that I hadn't brought any *Heep Hop* with me to Mongolia. He was constantly asking to listen to the handful of rap that I had on my mp3 player, and I could see that even though he didn't understand any of the words, he somehow understood the songs better than I did.

Little Davasuren – the thousand-superballs-in-a-blender Davaa - was a perfect balance of innocence and smugness. Habitually garbed in pigtails and sweatpants, she possessed a MacGyver-like ability to improvise games with bits of rubbish that she found in the yard. She was also a perpetual line-crosser, and constantly pushed the license of her precociousness. In those first few weeks, she made a game of sneaking into my room whenever I was away, filching from the candy stash in my top desk drawer and snapping random pictures with my digital camera. (Whenever I would check the memory card on my camera, I would inevitably find dozens of blurry, unfocused shots of ankles, table legs and foreheads.)

And then there was my host father, Chuluun.

He was a thin and wiry man, but had huge, calloused hands which he would constantly wring together whenever he spoke. His face was slightly sunken, his nose slightly crooked, his cheeks slightly stubby, his humor slightly crass, his moods slightly menacing.

He smelled like vodka dumped in a kitty litter box.

A former employee of the Altan Dornod Mongol mining corporation, Chuluun had been laid off when the local mine ran dry and the company left Delgerkhovd for yellower pastures. Now - like many other unemployed Delgerkhovd men - he was working as a private farmer, living in the countryside outside town for weeks on end, tending to the meager Dansaran crops, while his family remained in the village surviving on Solo's income as school librarian. But every now and then Chuluun would return to the village, like a moth returning to a floodlight, and make a clumsy attempt at taking charge of things again.

The first time I met him, he was stinking drunk.

He came back from the countryside late on a Wednesday night – three days after I had first arrived in Delgerkhovd - hours after I had gone to sleep. It turned out that nobody else was expecting him back that night either, and the rest of the family was just as surprised as I was when Chuluun announced his triumphant return with an unholy pounding on the front door and booze-addled shouts of *"HOOOOEEEEEYYY!"*

I pulled on a t-shirt and opened my door to investigate.

Solo was already up and apologizing to me, as she briskly walked to the door to let her husband in. The Dansaran boys and Little Davaa were up as well, rubbing sleep out of their eyes, indebted by custom to greet their father upon his return.

As soon as the door was unlocked, Chuluun burst into the kitchen, the resplendent light of the Mongolian moon in his wake. An average man in height and stature, he moved like he was drunk even when he was sober. One of his eyes was a sickly pink from some sort of infection he'd gotten in the countryside, and it glinted in the moonlight like a ruby as he entered the room. He carried two, five-gallon jugs in his hands, one full of homemade vodka and another filled with *aairag* (fermented horse milk), a traditional Mongol alcohol that can approach 40 proof.

Setting his jugs of booze down on the table, Chuluun grabbed Solo by the waist and swept her up in an embrace as she scolded him lightly in Mongolian. When their hug was over, I went to shake my host father's hand, but was quickly swept up in an embrace as well, receiving my first traditional Mongolian greeting as Chuluun brought his face up to mine and took deep sniffs of both my cheeks.

As soon as he set me down, Chuluun grabbed a couple of glasses from the kitchen shelf and unscrewed the caps of his liquor jugs. He poured me a shot of vodka which I tried to politely refuse, but as I was beginning to learn, one does not refuse alcohol in Mongolia so easily.

"Thank you, but I'm tired," I objected in English. "And that vodka looks dirty as hell, man... *bayarlaa... okhgui.*"

"*Neg... Neg...*" Chuluun insisted, holding up his index finger.

"Fine," I capitulated, remembering the Corps' advice about drinking in Mongolia. "One shot, you bastard."

Three shots of vodka later, Chuluun switched to the *aairag* jug, and poured me out a heaping glass of the effervescent horse milk. It tasted like old yogurt mixed with cheap sparkling wine, and as I would find out when I woke up the next morning, is well-known in Mongolia for being a natural laxative.

"Do you like it?" he asked me in Mongolian, eyeing me curiously.

"It's the goddamn bees' knees alright," I said in English, grimacing and nodding.

Decorum required that I give him a gift in return. I had already given out all of my little souvenirs from America by then, but I had saved a carton of Camel Lights for special situations. Running back to my bedroom, I grabbed the carton and gave it to my host father. He thanked me, tore open the carton and extracted a pack, then offered me a cigarette. Taking the smoke graciously (with my right hand, as custom dictated), we went outside to light up.

The sky was clear that night, a thousand times deeper than the Hayden Planetarium could ever aspire to emulate, and a million stars silhouetted a fat, almost-bursting moon. We leaned against the side of the house and puffed on our cigarettes, not saying a word, until Chuluun pointed up at the stars.

"*Look,*" he said in Mongolian.

I peeked to where his calloused finger jabbed the air, seeing nothing.

"*Kharach! Kharach!*" he repeated, raising his voice.

"*Oilgogkhgui,*" I said, shaking my head. "I don't understand you, dude."

Chuluun rolled his eyes, and made a sound like an airplane. "*America... danda... ongotz. Danda...*"

And finally I realized that he wasn't pointing to what *was* there, he was pointing to what *wasn't*... airplanes. It was a virgin sky, absent of any manmade pollution, absent of satellites and jet airliners, fifty million points of light shining down from above... and not one of them an airplane.

It was the sky from my dreams, no doubt.

It was the reason I came to Mongolia.

"Nothing," I told my host father, nodding that I understood. "*Bayarlaa.*"

"*Zuger,*" he said, his pinked right eye rosy and slightly mad in the moonlight. "*Zuger zuger.*"

***

As it turned out, "*Zuger*" was the most important word I would learn during my entire stay in Delgerkhovd.

The Mongolian use of Zuger is one of the most flexible of any language in the world, the only rival being the modern American use of FUCK. The word transcends labels such as "verb" or "noun", instead opting into that special class of vocabulary that can be used in any desired way, at any desired time, well beyond the normal rules of grammar. Zuger can mean: "It's okay", "Don't Worry", "I Agree", "You're Welcome", "I Concede", "Be Well", "Relax", "Good Job" or "That's the Way Things Go", among many other conjugations and amalgams.

But the power of the word extends well beyond linguistics. Zuger is a way of life, a pattern of assumptions on the same wavelength as any classical concept of Zen, a happy-go-lucky and fatalistic philosophy that is common in places the world considers poor. It is a way to accept failure, as much as it is to celebrate fortune. *Zuger,* the crops failed... *Zuger,* no money for new shoes... *Zuger,* the well water is getting browner... *Zuger,* the hospitals are full... *Zuger,* there's hopelessness in the air... *Zuger*, the world is unfair... *Zuger*, we're drowning... *Zuger*, the end is nigh.

Zuger... it's not that big a deal, because there is love.

To survive as an American in Mongolia, it is crucial that one understands the concept of Zuger.

Consider the following example.

The Dansaran's home, like almost all of rural Mongolia, was overrun with monster blackflies each summer. The bastards were without mercy, superhuman in their tenacity and daring, and massive in number to boot. They would land on my face while I slept and drown in my soup when I ate. There would be dozens of them in any room at any given time, a plague of Biblical proportions, a burden on the sanity of any first world citizen.

Solo had hung up some fly strips throughout the house, but fly strips are expensive on a Delgerkhovd budget and I knew that she was only doing it as a luxury for me. To deal with the insect scourge in the meanwhile, Solo had constructed a half-dozen, homemade fly swatters out of bamboo poles and spare strips of rubber she'd found lying around the village. Elegant in their simplicity, the bamboo swatters were amazingly well balanced, and when I held one in my hand I felt like I was grasping a finely crafted ninja weapon.

Whenever the fly population grew beyond tolerance, the family and I would each grab a swatter and go on a massive, hour-long hunt. It was as if we were a platoon of mighty Mongol Zen warriors, on the hunt for demons. Deftly we crashed our swatters upon the heads and bodies of the bastard flies, waltzing around the house in an improvised ballet of murder.

WHACK! WHACK! WHACK! WHACK! WHACK!

Death was never more beautiful.

Each family member had his or her own particular style. Solo used grand, arcing blows like a dancer... Nyam had a no-nonsense technique meant to allow him to make the maximum amount of strikes... Bymba would ham it up and use Hollywood-esque attacks (posing and screaming like Bruce Lee)... and Davaa specialized in the flies that landed low to the ground. Even Chuluun joined in once in a while, whenever he was home and sober.

Together, we were a spinning dervish of a fly snuff squad, a clan of insect assassins, an unconquerable bug Ragnarok. We wouldn't stop until the entire house was covered with fly guts, and we had a gargantuan heap of bodies on the floor. When the carnage was over, we'd stand victorious over the slaughter, truly and deeply feeling as if we'd done something good and sacred.

And inevitably, the house would be filled with flies again a few hours later.

Zuger.

***

After a few weeks, life in Delgerkhovd finally started to settle down, and I developed my own happy-holy morning routine... the first manifestation of the Zuger mind.

I would wake up with the sun, usually having beaten my alarm clock to the punch, something I couldn't ever recall doing in New Jersey. I'd roll out of bed to find the Dansarans already up and active: Solo stirring a pot of milk-tea on the mudroom stove, Davaa playing outside in the yard, and Nyam and Bymba in the living room, watching the fuzzy, rabbit-eared, black and white television (that could only pick up MNB, the national propaganda station.)

After my morning trip to the outhouse, I'd come back inside and wash my hands and face in the dry sink, using a saucepan full of water from the family supply. The water would be stiff and cold, and would instantly wake me as I'd splash it against my stubbly cheeks. While waiting for breakfast, I'd fill my Corps-issued water distiller with a fresh gallon and set it to work. I had set the distiller up on a little plastic stool that the Dansarans had bought for me, and whenever I filled it up, I felt like I was standing before a tiny shrine praying for water... my own little morning baptism.

With immaculate timing on the part of Solo, breakfast would appear on the table ten minutes before I left for Peace Corps language and culture training. The meals were always sparse but filling: a bowl of farina, *suutey bodha* (rice-milk), or sometimes just a big hunk of homemade bread and butter. Solo had noticed that I went nuts over *gambir* - fried and sugared flatbread - so there was always a lidded colander full of the stuff on the kitchen table. I'd drink my morning tea all ritual-like, stirring three sugar cubes in the steaming cup one at a time, and then taking increasingly larger sips in ratio with the golden mean. After I finished, I'd place the used tea bag on a small porcelain saucer to be used again the next day, say goodbye to my host family, then pick up my things and go to my Peace Corps training classes until the evening: the Human Ourobouros.

I'd leave the house in a happy silence - like a slightly sleepy monk going fishing - and the sky would unfailingly be bright and portentous. Instead of walking along the main path - as most of the other Delgerkhovd Seven did - I would take a long, roundabout route through an open field on the edge of our bagh. Sometimes I'd hum little pieces of traditional folk songs that I'd overheard Solo or Davaa singing that morning, but above all, my world would be wonderfully hushed and patient, with no car horns or highway breezes, only the sound of my boots crunching over the dirt and the lull of my breath. And gradually, I began to forget the reason that I'd come to Mongolia.

***

To understand Delgerkhovd, one must understand the River.

The lifeblood of Delgerkhovd, the Kharaa River was about a half-mile walk from the center of town. It was a gorgeous spread of clear water with a dreamy, grassy shoreline, the kind of thing that you see on the covers of romance novels. During the afternoon's warm hours there would always be dozens of villagers gracing its banks - swimming, washing clothes, bathing and fishing in an endless tessellation of activity.

We didn't have training sessions on the weekend, so if the weather was good, I'd go down to the river and bum around in the sunshine. I'd take my dirty laundry, plastic washing basin, a bar of soap and a baggie full of powdered laundry detergent (that I bought at the delguur), and hike downstream until I found a waist-deep and secluded part of the river. There, I'd set up my things on a flat spot by the riverbank, take my socks off, and dip my feet in the water, until I understood the essence of the river that day.

I'd never washed clothes by hand before in my life, but the process was pretty straightforward. I'd fill my basin with river water and lug it over to the shore, then pour in some laundry detergent and swish it around to foam it up. Socks were usually the top priority, so I'd do those first, tossing them in the basin and rubbing them together briskly to get the dirt off. I'd lay the washed socks down on the grass to dry in the sun, then I'd do my small travel towel, t-shirts, spare blue jeans, and finally my underwear, laying everything out neatly on the grass to dry. I'd dump the leftover water - now opaque and scummy - away from the river like I'd seen the other villagers do.

While my clothes dried, I'd strip down to my boxers and wade into the river with my bar of soap. The water would rush downstream around my chest and make it tricky to stand up, so I'd have to do this weird and funny flamingo dance as I lifted my body parts out of the river to soap them up. Watching the soap bubbles eddy away on the current, I felt like a little boy in the grandest bathtub of all. When I was done bathing I'd float around for awhile, suspended in the current with my arms outstretched and my feet together for balance. A river bath leaves a gritty and unique consistency on the skin, a second layer of flesh, and I'd never really emerge from a bath totally clean.

But who was I trying to impress, anyway?

Later that summer, I'd end up purchasing a cheap plastic inner tube from the bottom shelf of one of the delguurs, and when the weather was right and I was in the mood, I'd go tubing on that beatific old river.

From town, I'd hike upstream about two or three miles - a good hour's ride – and pick a good launching spot. The inner tube was small - for children, really - and also bright neon orange, with pictures of little ducks all over it. Children would come running to gape and laugh at me as I floated past, a floating fool's armada. I'd laugh with them and wave hello, then soar off on a fresh current.

They were God-inspiring experiences, my little tubing so-jurns... the mosaic shimmering of the water in the mid-day sun, small fish leaping up from the ripples in synchronized patterns, Mongol children running up to laugh kindly at me as I floated past, befuddled horses and sheep and goats lifting their heads from the water, the cool of the water on my legs and the healing sunshine on my torso, and always the gorgeous sky, with its huge, bulbous sun that made everything else in the world seem so insignificant.

The Delgerkhovd river was a special place for me, and as I floated downstream in my tube, I couldn't help but think of Siddhartha, sitting there at *his* special place, on *his* special river, floating on *his* ass just like I was.

After all, even Buddha was once a useless bum.

***

But then, barely five weeks after I arrived in Delgerkhovd – just as I had finally settled in - that all changed forever.

It was after sunset, and I was writing at my desk when a knock came on my bedroom door. This was my first clue that something was wrong... Mongolians never knock at the entrances of friends and family, they simply enter.

"*Nashaa*," I said, putting my notebook aside. "Come in."

To my surprise, the entire family Dansaran was there, their heads cast downwards in some secret shame. Solo stood in front, her Peace Corps-issued dictionary tucked under her arm, wringing her chubby hands together nervously. Chuluun stood next to her, remaining motionless, his hands thrust helplessly in his pockets. The Dansaran children stood behind their parents, Davaa with dried tear trails on her quieted face, and Bymba and Nyam looking like cocker-spaniels that got caught chewing up a Donatello statue.

"To talk?" Solo asked tentatively in English.

The family waited for my reply.

"Talk... yes...*yarcen ve?*" I asked them, trying to keep my voice level, afraid that I would frighten them away like fish if I spoke too loudly. "What happened?"

Solo reached into her pocket and pulled out a small, colorful wad of bills, placing the money ball on my desk where it sat like an origami swan. She immediately stepped back, never taking her eyes from mine.

I looked at the money... then back up at my host family... then at the money again.

And a moment of self-conscious silence passed, as it dawned on me what had happened.

The Corps gave us each 20,000 Mongolian tugrugs - about 20 dollars - as a monthly allowance during training, more than enough for cigarettes and an occasional cold-water shower at the village bathhouse. I usually had a little money left over each month, so I'd buy my host family some cookies and chocolate at a delguur or slip the kids a few tugrugs, although the Corps discouraged that sort of thing.

"At all costs, avoid letting your neighbors think that you have extra amounts of money laying around," the Corps staff told us back at Camp Chingiis.

Now I saw why.

"It's ok..." I said, quickly sweeping the money up and putting it in my pocket so it would be out of sight. "*Zuger zuger.*"

I knew the answer to my next question before I asked it. "Who stole the money? *Khen be?*"

Upon hearing my question, Chuluun's head snapped up, although he still wouldn't look me in the eye. He said noth-ing, but I understood the story immediately... Solo had caught Chuluun stealing my allowance money, and was making him give it back.

And to punish him, she had told the children what he had done.

"I see," I said softly, nodding that I understood.

"Eric..." said a voice. "Eric..."

I looked over at Nyam. The teenager raised and lowered an imaginary bottle to his lips.

"*Aairag... Vodka*," he told me, looking at Chuluun as he said the words, as his father blanched with shame.

After a moment, Solo rustled through her dictionary.

"Thief..." she told me, pointing at the words with a stabbing finger. "Steal. Apology. Ashamed."

"Hey," I said, cutting her off as she searched through the dictionary for more words, "it's not a big deal. *Zuger.*"

Trying to prove that I wasn't lying, I took the money wad and tried to hand it to Chuluun. "Here you go," I said stupidly, not realizing what I was doing, acting on some gross and unconscious American instinct.

Chuluun recoiled, terrified at the prospect of taking my money.

"*Chattangui, chattangui,*" he insisted, shaking his head like I was offering him hot coals.

I glanced down at little Davaa - who was sniffling in the doorway - and smiled to cheer her up. I extended her a couple of the bills. "Would you like a few bucks, then, Davaa?"

As soon as I held out the money, she began to bawl. *Jesus,* I thought, feeling like a monkey trying to do surgery with a butter knife.

"*Moe,*" Davaa sobbed, extending her pinky downward in shame. "*Moe aav...*"

"*Zuger...*" I insisted weakly, stealing a look over at Solo.

"*Zuger beesh,*" insisted Solo, gathering up Davaa and hushing her. "Bad."

Chuluun shrunk back a step, cringing at the word. There was a long silence then, until Solo picked up her dictionary.

"Peace Corps... grievance?" Solo questioned, pointing at words in the book one-by-one with a painful slowness. "Live... new... family?"

The Dansarans waited for my answer, five pairs of eyes fixed upon me.

"No," I said immediately, "*Ugui*. It's our little... um... *nu-utz*," I said, pointing at the Mongolian word for "secret" in the dictionary.

I turned to look at Chuluun. He wobbled weakly and meekly, like a drunk who's been socked in the gut.

"*Oochlaray*," he apologized, briefly meeting my eyes, then immediately casting his gaze downward. "*Oochlaray*."

"*Zuger*," I said. "It's just money, after all, dude."

After a long silence, I told the Dansarans that I was tired. They took the hint, wished me goodnight, and left me alone at my desk.

And that was that.

The next day, Solo went to the delguur and bought a padlock with a single key, and together, we screwed a hinge on the outer edge of my bedroom door. Afterwards, my room was always locked when I was out of the house, and that was the last time any of us ever brought the theft up again.

But deep down I think that we all knew something had changed, because from that point on, there was a knock on my door... every... single... time.

$$\sim 5 \sim$$

The Hood Ornament and The Quitter

I'm sure that the blind altruism of those first few weeks would have worn off soon anyway.

There was sunburn and mosquitoes and dandruff, to be sure. There was the terrible water with its crust and dirt, and bits of hair, fur and giardia. There were the weird smells, the endless meals of fat and flour, the rotten outhouses... an entire universe of absurdities and discomforts. But in the end, it wasn't these exchanges of material comforts – tendering a mattress for a plank - that made me start dreading to roll out of bed in the morning.

It was my cultural enfeeblement.

It was a weird and sad thing to be waited upon like I was some sort of foreign prince, especially when I had come to Mongolia to save *them*. And although I often tried to explain this to the Dansarans, the words would always end up coming out wrong. Everywhere I looked I was dependant - the Corps, my host family, the safety bubble of our little volunteer circle. I had to relearn how to cook, how to clean, how to bathe, how to eat, how to wash.

I was a child again.

Worse yet, I had become a hood ornament - a Christmas display in a windowsill - and it was beginning to hurt to walk around all day with a smile on my face. Any time I took out my guitar to practice a few scales, I would suddenly find myself putting on a forced concert for three children and a wandering herder. Whenever I walked outside to take a dump, I could hear the neighbors whispering about me, wondering if mine looked like theirs. Even when I closed my eyes, I could feel the gazes sweeping over me, the endless pokes and tastes and sniffs. A million restless eyeballs were fixated on me at all times... some gracious, some proud, some playful, some angry, but all curious.

And I couldn't be a jerk to a single pair of them.

I had lost the precious bubble of privacy that I'd gotten used to in America and it was driving me mad. I was an over-mellowed cantaloupe on a supermarket shelf, fingered too many times to be appealing to anybody anymore. For better or worse, no other nation on Earth will allow a human being to fall through the cracks of society like America. And for the first time in my life, I was beginning to realize how much I needed that.

The great Jack London once wrote that the paramount challenge one faces in a far country is in learning to adapt the mind's attitude towards one's own hopelessly fixed habits. "It is better for the man who cannot fit himself to the new groove to return to his own country," Ol' Jack wrote. "For if he delay too long, he will surely die."

But over those early days, as life in rural Mongolia began to reveal its true self, it wasn't only things like this that got to me. What really got me was a gradual and troubling realization... I *hadn't* escaped the capricious minutiae of life that I thought I had kicked to the curb that night in Los Angeles so long ago. Instead, I had simply replaced my old problems and frustrations with new ones, exchanged one culture which I didn't understand for another which I understood even less.

I was still the same person. The world was still the same place.

And neither of us understood each other any better than when I was languishing in America.

***

The other volunteers had their own problems.

Vinko had become the injury magnet of the group. Only a day after arriving in Delgerkhovd, he nearly gave himself a concussion when he forgot to duck and smashed his head on the doorway in Ray's ger. Two weeks later, he sliced a huge gash in his hand when he fell down the local holy mountain on a solo hike. He was forever showing up with ungodly bruises, burns and other wounds, and under the orders of the Peace Corps-Mongolia medical director, he had begun to carry around a roll of emergency gauze in his backpack wherever he went.

Bridget - who had probably never had a curfew in her life - had been almost comically matched with overbearing host parents, who insisted that Bridget tell them where she would be (and who she would be with) at all times. Bridget responded to this demand by disappearing for long stretches of time without warning, then showing up at one of our houses piss drunk in the middle of the night, screeching and guffawing about some secret joke that only she understood.

It was the same with the others.

Ray was the first of us to come down with the "Delgerkhovd Squirts" when he drank unfiltered water by mistake. Eddie lost a $300 camera lens down the hole of an outhouse. Abbie, a vegetarian in America, lost 5 pounds off her already tiny frame because "everything in Mongolia has MEAT!!! in it."

And on and on it went.

***

One afternoon I went over to visit Abbie, looking to see if she might lend me her copy of The Brothers Karamozov. I found her sitting outside on the porch muttering to herself, a Swiss Army knife in her hand. I knew that Abbie was especially fond of her knife, a nice outdoorsy hippie-model that she must have spent a couple hundred dollars on, and whose blade never touched flesh... only art and plants.

Which is why it surprised me to see her knife handle covered in a sticky, coagulated, crimson mess, with little, glistening, organic bits wedged in between the blades.

"Holy shit," I said, looking around for signs of struggle. "Did you kill somebody, dude?"

"I'm a pacifist, remember?" she asked, shaking her head. "But I'm thinking that over as we speak."

She emitted a tiny, forced laugh and held out the knife for me to see.

"What's that stuff there?" I asked, pointing to the ugly, crimson residue.

"IT'S FUCKING BLOOD!" the little Buddha-skater-girl exploded, and for a second I was shocked into abject silence.

"My host brother asked if he could use my knife today, used it to skin a sheep, and didn't even bother to wipe the fucking blood off! He just handed the thing back to me and took off. My host parents are away in the khuudo, and my knife looks like murder, and on top of it all I'm soooooo hungry..."

She stopped talking, her words trailing off at the mention of hunger.

"Man," I said after a moment, "How did Ghandi and Cesar Chavez do it, huh?"

We sat there for a minute in silence.

"You know," Abbie said at last, "Sometimes I think that I should have just stayed at home in Portland and volunteered for the local ACLU. Maybe I could have done a lot more good back there, where things made sense."

"Nah, we belong out here," I lied.

"Hey, can I ask you a question?" she said, as if she hadn't heard me. "Tell me honestly... can you picture yourself doing this for two years?"

I looked at Abbie. I looked away. I looked back at Abbie.

What else could I have said but yes?

***

One morning at school while waiting for language class to start, Ralph and I were standing around, smoking cigarettes and throwing the bullshit. We were the first ones to arrive for class that morning, the only time I can remember that ever happening... in either of our cases.

When I was done with my cigarette, I ground the butt into the dirt and put it back in my cigarette pack, as I'd gotten in the habit of doing.

"What'd you do that for?" asked Ralph, watching me and scratching at the stubble on his face.

When I told him that it seemed like a shame to dirty the village up, Ralph just laughed.

"Look around you, E. The whole village is filthy already,' he said, and of course he was right, there were cigarette butts and broken glass and all sorts of debris everywhere, not only at the school, but all through the village wherever people had lived or traveled.

"Why are you getting so weepy about throwing one more butt on the ground?" Ralph continued. "Really, isn't it like pissing in a public pool at this point?"

I told him that I was trying to set a good example.

"Yeah right," he snorted, chuckling like a goon.

"I mean it, man," I told him, a little pissed off. "I know that you're just here for a work reference, but some of us are trying to save the world."

Ralph looked at me and cocked an eyebrow. "Yeah? Well, maybe I'm the only honest one here... except maybe for Bridget. You don't fool me, E. You've got your own secret motive for being here that has nothing to do with saving the world, just like the rest of us. I can see it in your face whenever you talk that philanthropic bullshit of yours. So what's the real reason that you're here, huh? What are you running from? What terrible guilt is making you pick up cigarette butts off the ground?"

And suddenly, I had nothing to say.

To his credit, Ralph let the whole thing drop, and didn't go out of his way to bum me out again. But somewhere inside, I knew that the fucker had hit upon something that had been creeping around my subconscious ever since I had first arrived in Mongolia, something that I had buried a long time ago and forgotten.

And it must have stuck in my head, because from that day on, I threw my cigarette butts wherever the hell I pleased.

***

In a few weeks we began our ESL teacher training, which took up most of our afternoons. As part of our training, the Corps had arranged for us to give the local schoolchildren free English lessons, so we spent the bulk of our afternoons doing practice teaching runs, testing out our half-baked lesson plans on the unsuspecting Delgerkhovd schoolchildren.

I had dabbled in the education field before joining the Corps, so the demoralizing world of teaching methodology was nothing new. But some of the other trainees had a harder time with it. Surprisingly, Ray - the professor's son - was the one really pulling his hair out over the whole thing.

You could tell he was embarrassed that he wasn't a better teacher, because of the way that he'd talked up his father... the former Peace Corps adventurer-turned university professor.

"Why isn't this working?" he griped to me outside one day during lunch break, after his class had failed yet again to grasp the concept of the past tense. He was on his second cigarette of the day.

Ray didn't smoke.

By invitation, I had sat in on one of Ray's classes and seen his problem... he was trying way too hard to befriend his students. It was a habit that cost him his credibility and control, and as a result, his students would start pouting whenever he tried to make them study.

"You can't keep trying to pal it up with your students, dude," I said.

"But I want them to like me," he protested.

"Are you here to make friends, or do some good?" I asked.

"Why can't it be both?"

I shook my head. "That's just the way it is, man. It's one or the other."

Ray leaned against the school wall and exhaled wearily. "That's the same thing that my dad always says."

"Sounds pretty wise."

Ray nodded. "He says that a lot, too."

***

I suppose it was only a matter of time before one of us reached the breaking point.

On August 7, less than a month before the end of PST, Ralph didn't show up for class. His host family didn't have a phone, so Chimgee walked to his home was while we waited outside the school. She came back an hour later with sad eyes, and told us that Ralph had decided to quit the Corps and go back to America.

Ralph left Delgerkhovd the next morning, chauffeured from the village in a Peace Corps Land Rover. We were drilling our post office vocabulary in language class, when he stopped in for a brief goodbye. Ralph wouldn't look anybody in the eye for more than a moment, and you could tell that he was ashamed of his decision, which I found funny because he so obviously hated Mongolia.

"I'm sorry," was all he said.

We all shook hands with our ex-brother and wished him luck, and that was the last any of us would ever hear from him.

After he was gone, Eddie told us that he'd been hanging out with Ralph at the river a few days before, and had caught wind of his plan to leave. Eddie said that he tried to talk him out of it, but Ralph just shook his head.

"All he would say was that 'Everything is the same everywhere'... over and over," Eddie said.

"What does that mean?" asked Abbie.

"Who cares?" replied Bridget.

Oyunn and Chimgee set us back to work on our vocabulary drills, but I couldn't concentrate, no matter how hard I tried.

So after a minute, I said that I had to use the outhouse and left class. Instead, I went around to the back of the building and lit a cigarette.

Ralph's departure had shaken us all, even though most of us wouldn't admit it. And suddenly, I had a terrible feeling that my "sacred routine" of the past few months was really only a rut... boredom mistaken for Zen. The truth was, my adrenaline tank had long ago been drained. The thrill was gone.

The beer goggles were off.

As I smoked and contemplated, I happened to glance down at the ground. There, among the dirt and shrub grasses, two insects were battling for their lives. As I watched, an ant struggled to haul a still-living beetle grub back to its colony on the other end of the schoolyard. In a desperate attempt to avoid its gruesome fate, the grub madly clung to anything within reach. In return, the ant contorted its pinchers and kept its frantic hold on the grub. *Who knows how long this battle has been going on*, I thought. *Maybe forever.*

It was an awful tug of war, and the end was nowhere in sight. The only humane thing to do was to intervene for one side or the other, and it was obvious what needed to be done... a mercy killing, *deus ex machina* style.

But as I bent down to do the deed, I realized that I had no clue which bug I should aid.

If I help the ant - I thought, looking down on them - *the grub will die a horrible and brutal death. But if I help the grub, some poor ant larvae will starve, and that's not right either.*

And I stood there, helpless in my own omnipotence, for a long time. Afraid to intervene, consumed with a silent horror that I couldn't quite understand, I watched the insects battle, doing nothing. Finally, with nothing resolved in my mind, I snubbed my cigarette out in the dirt and returned to class, leaving the ant and the grub to sort things out themselves.

Sometimes the world is just too large... sometimes there is nothing to say... sometimes we can't make a difference.

Sometimes, we don't need to.

Zuger, zuger.

$$\sim 6 \sim$$

Marijuana Gorge

As I passed the 60-day mark, life continued in Delgerkhovd.

In an attempt to keep my spirits high, I had been going on bi-weekly hikes through the nearby mountains. The mountains were pretty things, low and rolling, more of a series of foothills than peaks. They were also secluded; a half-hour hike would lead me out beyond human contact, where the only footprints I would see would be my own. There was twenty miles in each direction between the next village over, which meant that there was no way that one person could see it all in three months.

It was in this vast khuudo that I discovered Marijuana Gorge.

It happened one day when I was solo hiking, a mile out of the village in the foothills of the Delgerkhovd Mountains. I was traveling alone, free of purpose, and the plains seemed extra green and luminous that day. Overhead, hawks and falcons rode the air currents like paper airplanes... solitary, figures on a silent horizon. The ground around me was dotted with small clusters of knotty bushes, and every now and then, I saw a fist-sized tunnel in the earth where a marmot had made its home.

As I walked, the sound of my boots echoed for miles, like shotgun blasts.

I had been following a nearby mountain ridge, which had been extending down at a gradual slope for a few hours. Now at last - a thousand feet away - the ridge ended, receding into a shallow ravine carved by centuries of rain runoff from the hills. As I got closer to the ravine, my eyes were drawn to a solitary birch tree rooted down below, a lonely stumpy thing, which stood out on the blank landscape like an emerald in the sky. I had been hiking for hours and the tree was a natural landmark, so I headed towards it, planning to rest in the shade and smoke a cigarette. But as I drew to within a few hundred feet, I noticed a familiar leaf shape from the corner of my eye which stopped me in my tracks, turning my hiking hums into a stunned silence.

It couldn't be, I thought. *I'm not that lucky.*

But sure enough, when I walked over to examine it, there it was... its foot-tall stalk jutting out from the earth... its seven, serrated leaves happy and green... its burgeoning stem healthy and lustrous, with tiny, gossamer buds on its splits.

Sure as shit, I had found a wild marijuana plant.

I had heard secondhand rumors that there was wild cannabis growing somewhere around the village, but hadn't paid them much credence. But now the proof was in front of me... and ready to harvest, to boot. Giddy with excitement, I began to search the area for other plants. Within a matter of minutes I had found dozens more, male and female, many taller and fuller bodied than my original find. They continued down to the ravine, so I gave a quick glance around and headed down to stake my claim.

In the ravine, a veritable shitload of plants had taken root, growth-exploding in a delightful fractal pattern, covering the entire interior of the ravine. There were hundreds of plants, maybe thousands, more than I could ever smoke in a summer... a pothead's Nirvana come to life. The whole thing was surreal, like a waking dream, something dreamed up in Hollywood and discarded as too unbelievable.

"Stoned Immaculate," I said to myself, and I guffawed for what seemed like hours.

I spent the rest of the day in the ravine - which I later dubbed Marijuana Gorge - walking around aimlessly and sniffing at the rows of plants before me. At last the sun started to sink low in the sky, and I realized that I had about two hours of light left to get back home. So I pinched off some of the larger buds, wrapped them up in cigarette cellophane, and jotted down the location of the ravine in my notebook. Then giving one last fond glance back at the gorge, I quickly began the hike back to Delgerkhovd.

"I'll be back," I shouted out to my new friends as I left for the village, my boots light with hope.

At home, I set the damp buds in an empty cardboard tea box to cure, which I then hid inside my closet. When the pot was finally dry enough to smoke, I went to a delguur and bought one of the huge sheets of uncut cigarette paper that Mongolians use to roll loose tobacco. I rolled my entire stash into a huge Tommy Chong-esque joint, then went out behind the Dansaran outhouse and lit the bugger up. I sucked the whole goddamn thing down in about two minutes, glancing over my shoulder to see if anyone was coming, like I was back in high school. It was terrible weed, choppy and harsh on the lungs, the kind of smoke that an unscrupulous dealer would cut with oregano and sell to an eighth grader.

But to this day, it's still the best joint I have ever smoked in my life.

The following Saturday, I spent noon to dusk at the ravine, harvesting handfuls of the tiny buds until my fingers were black and gooey. When it finally started to get dark I had more than six ounces of pot.

From that point on, the rest of my stay in Delgerkhovd was a little different.

In the evenings, I'd roll huge spliffs and climb the mountain next to our hashaa bagh to watch the sun set. Perched cross-legged on a boulder, I'd puff on my cigar-sized joints and look out on the village with a lazy detachment, feeling like a hermit living on the edge of Time. The beautiful, purple sunsets would soak into me like wine into a sponge, and any of the countless little hiccups and disappointments of the day would float away like plumes of smoke.

At times like these, I would think about how very lucky I was to experience God in the ways I have. I thought about poor Solo, who might live the rest of her life without ever seeing an ocean. Or little Davaa, who might never eat a taco. Or brother Nyam, who might never smoke a joint in his life.

And on my mountain, I felt sorry for them - not just for the Dansarans - but for all those poor fuckers throughout the world... all those unfortunate bastards who would never realize that they were in Nirvana, simply because they'd had the misfortune of being born there.

~ 7 ~

The Moving Sidewalk

The next few weeks passed slowly.

In old Mongolia, time operates like a muzzy heroin addict on a moving sidewalk. "Mongol Time" is a broken yo-yo... a bent Slinky... a deck with missing cards. It softens the reflexes at the same time it sharpens the instincts. It liquefies your day.

You wake up earlier, but slower. You stop crossing off the days on your calendar. You forget what day of the week it is. Weeks pass like broken-wing butterflies. Months disappear like soap bubbles down a drain.

And before you know it... BAM!... you're done.

***

Pre-Service Training ended on August 12, three weeks before my twenty-fifth birthday.

When it was all said and done, here's how my official Peace Corps resume looked: 185 hours of Mongolian language training, 50 hours of cross-cultural training, and 140 hours of ESL methodology training. But those limp compilations of numbers could only begin to hint at the real-world education that I had received in Delgerkhovd. I had spent my three months in Purgatory; I had paid my dues.

And I had smiled all the way through them.

As for the Dansarans and I, there wasn't any teary farewell. Mongolians don't believe in such things. But my host family and I knew the truth of the matter... in all likelihood, we'd never see each other again.

We said our goodbyes the night before I left for Ulaanbaatar, the staging point for all new volunteer departures. The cucumbers from the Dansarans' garden had finally grown big enough to pick, and we spent a long time casually munching on these as we sat outside in the yard, basking in the glorious Mongol night. The air that night was slightly cold and snappish, like the first bite into a refrigerated apple. The stars were also particularly bright that evening, and to make conversation, Solo asked me if I knew the names of any constellations.

"Sure," I asserted in my fractured Mongolian, my mouth full of cucumber. "But we have different names for them in America."

I proceeded to point at arbitrary groups of stars, connecting imaginary lines with my index finger while looking up random vocabulary in my dictionary. "This is Grandma's Triangle over there in the south. And there's the Great Disease... the Broken Sandwich... Jimbo the Dishwasher. And there, over in the northeast, is my favorite... the Magic Toilet."

"Yes, I can see that one!" exclaimed Little Davaa, squinting her eyes in sudden seriousness.

"If you see it, it is there," said Solo in Mongolian, patting her daughter on the head and smiling at me.

We all sat silently for a while then, finishing off the cucumbers and listening to the sounds of the village after hours... barking dogs, crickets, and the sound of the wind in the grass. But at last the moon began to crest, and we all began to yawn. Sensing that it was time to call it quits, Solo stood up and announced that it was time to give me my "farewell gifts."

"Oh man, that's not necessary," I said, trying to be polite.

Solo waved me off. "*Bedgie bedgie*," she said, disappearing inside. A minute later, she emerged with a plastic bag full of presents, and the Dansarans gathered around me ceremoniously in the splendid moonlight. First, Solo dug into the bag and produced a new *khaadad*. She held the blue length of cloth out in her hands to me, explaining in her simplest Mongolian that the fabric represented the sky, which would always be over me as long as I lived in Mongolia.

"*Bayarla*," I said, accepting the ceremonial cloth with open palms like it was a samurai sword.

When the exchange was done, Solo reached into the bag and handed me a hand-sewn Mongolian *tsampt*... a traditional shirt. The tsampt was a powder blue color, shiny and sharp, with delicate silver trim cascading down the hems. I turned her gift over in my hands, feeling the silky material in my palms. It was like something that a Hollywood brahma would wear.

Over the past week, I had caught glimpses of Solo making my gifts, but I was still surprised by how beautiful the craftsmanship turned out, and I told her so.

"*Bayarlaa*," I told my host family, bowing slightly.

"Zuger," Solo told me.

"Zuger," repeated her children.

"Zuger," repeated Chuluun.

I slept on the living room floor with the rest of the family that night, my luggage packed and piled in a heap next to me. We were hobos whiling away the night in the Grand Central subway station... hamsters scrunching in a litter pile... atoms vibrating in the same molecule.

And that was the last I ever saw of the Dansarans.

***

Back in Ulaanbaatar, the Corps finally got around to revealing our permanent assignments. Most of us had gotten what they wanted... or deserved.

Eddie had been stationed near the most iconic body of water in Mongolia, Lake Khuvsgul, with the Reindeer People of the northern tundras. Ray had been stationed in one of the local *aimag* centers – Mongolia's equivalent of the "satellite city"- where he was given the task of running the English prep program at one of the city's secondary schools. Abbie had ended up with an assignment as a community-building specialist in Khentii, a rural province in the far Eastern plains of Mongolia. Vinko the adventurer had been assigned to Baganolgii, a last-stop village near the southern Dundgobi desert-steppe. And Bridget had been assigned to a post in Ulaanbaatar, where she could teach English from the relative comfort of the city, home to so many of her vices.

As for myself, I had asked the Corps to send me to the gnarliest site they had... the "old school" Peace Corps experience. They replied by giving me an assignment in a tiny village called Mandalzuud, way out on the fringes of the infamous Gobi Desert. The way the Corps described it, Mandalzuud was a perfect microcosm of old Mongolia – rustic, rural, and even poorer than Delgerkhovd:

A population of 2,350 people and 100,000 livestock. No internet or cell phone reception. No running water. Electricity prone to blackouts. High unemployment rate. Stagnating drinking wells. No fuel, except for coal and dried dung. No jobs, except for raising sheep or drying dung.

It was exactly what I had asked for, a place where I could really make an impact. It was a place where every crappy English teacher is an instant master of foreign languages, and everyone who knows how to read the label on a bottle of Tylenol is a health expert. It was a chance to save the world, or die trying.

But more importantly, it was a chance to find the answer to the question that had brought me to Mongolia in the first place... the question that had started me on this whole two-year path to redemption ... WHAT IS THE VALUE OF ONE GOOD DEED?

Because God help me, I sure as hell hadn't found any answers in Mongolia yet.

And time was steadily running out.

END, PART ONE

$$\sim 8 \sim$$

<u>**Intermission**</u>

Many Mongolian herders say that *Allgkhoi Khorkhoy* – the Mongolian Death Worm - is the most dangerous thing in the Gobi Desert.

Stretched out to its full length, the herders say, the *Allgkhoi Khorkhoy* - the "Intestine Worm" - can strike fear into the hearts of even the stoutest *Naadam* warrior. The giant worm can grow to the size of two men, maybe three, depending on who you ask and how drunk they are. Like a serpent from Hell, the beast is blood-red in color, and gives off a foul stench that reminds many of rotten flesh. When it attacks, it fights with the anger of a hundred wolves. Inside the worm's terrible mouth lies a thousand teeth, and each tooth is the equal of a thousand, tiny knives.

Nothing that feels its bite ever survives.

The Mongolian Death Worm is subterranean, hibernating underground for most of the year. But every summer in June and July, just when the weather is at its hottest, the worm emerges from its slumber... hungry... impatient.

And nothing in the Gobi is safe.

Many more "respectable" witnesses call the Death Worm a local myth... a product of a fantasy-prone and backwards culture... a totem on par with Bigfoot, or the Loch Ness Monster, or El Chupacabra. But get a couple of vodka shots into a herder and he'll tell you different.

Some herders say that the Death Worm can change its color like a chameleon, and sneak up on its prey, concealed in the shifting sands. Others insist that the worm can spew forth a corrosive acid attack from its mouth, spraying any doomed creature within a twenty foot radius. Still others attest that the beast can give off a killer electrical discharge like an eel, or that the worm can kill by mere touch alone.

Nobody knows who is right.

Maybe they all are.

Some call the *Allgkhoi Khorkhoy* the Mongolian embodiment of Death... a rolling incarnation of the old ways... a reminder of our own fragile mortality. Some even say that the beast can appear in one's dreams. Some say this, and some say that, and some are content to merely sit and listen to the tales get out of hand, once again.

But almost everyone agrees on one thing.

It's no goddamn spirit animal... that's for sure.

~ 9 ~

PART TWO

**MANDALZUUD, DUNDGOBI PROVINCE
(ONE MONTH LATER)**

<u>Waking to Beetles</u>

It was the crack of dawn one morning in late September, when I woke to discover that my *ger* tent was infested with thousands of desert beetles.

Again.

I suppose that I shouldn't have left the lamp on all night. That was *my* mistake. The little bastards had found the damn thing irresistible; it had probably been the only artificial light around for miles. Less than a centimeter wide, the tiny desert beetles were capable of struggling through the holes in a mosquito net, which meant that they had no problem finding their way through the folds of my ger. Everywhere I looked there were beetles... crawling, clinging or spinning on their backs... tiny, drunken turtles... ecstatic to have finally reached the mysterious glow... the blessed source... the Big

Secret in the Sky... click... click... clack... click... clack... clack... click... clack... click... click... clack... click... clack... clack... click... clack...

Finally, with a huge sigh, I got out of bed and turned off my lamp.

It took me about half an hour to sweep up the majority of the beetles with my broom and pan, but many were so deeply dug into my rug that I couldn't get at them. Finally, in a fit of frustration, I tore off some strips of duct tape and wrapped them around my hands like mittens, then tromped around the ger and slapped up the remaining beetles with my improvised flypaper.

What a hell of a thing to have to do at seven in the morning, I thought, my death mittens growing heavy with corpses. *I bet that Ghandi and Mother Theresa never had to put up with this.*

When I was finally finished, I set a kettle of water boiling on my hotplate and went outside to take my morning piss. And as I urinated on a patch of thankful desert grass – kill a thousand and save one - I gazed out at my new home with wonder and hatred in my heart...

Mandalzuud.

***

I'd like to write that the village of Mandalzuud was a place of natural beauty and virgin desert, a place of rebirth and mysticism... but that's not really true.

It was more like a colony of Mongolians had landed on Mars, and built a huge trailer park.

While it wasn't exactly "the middle of nowhere" (like I had specifically requested), Mandalzuud was still *way the fuck out there*. The village is part of the Dundgobi province, one of the most remote in all of Mongolia, which lies about 200 kilometers from the heart of the infamous Gobi Desert. It is surrounded by fifty miles of desert steppe - much like a dry island – where the summers are broiling dry and the winters are among the coldest on Earth.

Outside the village, the terrain is barren, save for a patchy network of reed-like grass, a marmot or two, the occasional saxaul bush and smattering of insects. Huge tracts of dusty, tan desert steppe stretch as far as the eyes can see, making one point on the horizon almost indistinguishable from another. In the far distance, a few small hills stand out like lumps in mashed potatoes, but all else is utterly flat except the sky, which looms so heavy overhead, that I was continually amazed that it didn't collapse. The air of the Dundgobi is bone dry, but also vicious and hungry, and the only colors for miles around are brown and blue.

Bob Ross could paint a landscape of it all in about a minute flat.

When I arrived, the Peace Corps' official population count for the village was 2,350, but the true size of Mandalzuud was about half of what that apocryphal number suggested. Overall, the village looked like the set of an old Hollywood western. The town buildings were tiny, square things - all in a general state of disrepair – each begging for paint, new windows or a wrecking ball. The gers were all meager and dilapidated – most of Mandalzuud's residents lived three or four to a tent - and even the nicer "homes" were little more than wooden shacks with delusions of grandeur. There wasn't a structure in town that had indoor plumbing.

It was like stepping two centuries back in time.

There was no cell phone reception anywhere in the village, and the closest Internet connection was fifty kilometers to the east. What little communication methods we had were shared by the entire community. For example, the Mandalzuud post office had one of only three telephone land lines in the village, the other two having been reserved for the bank and the government building. As such, the post office was the incoming and outgoing line for a thousand villagers... the only "pay phone" in town.

I would end up writing a lot of letters during my stay.

The village's grip on electricity was likewise tenuous. Mandalzuud was connected to the national power grid, which ran along the main bus route leading to U.B. This single master power line - on which every other line in the village relied upon - ran through several hundred kilometers of empty steppe between villages. Built with inferior materials and exposed to the sand, sun, cold and wind of the Gobi, most sections of the power line had an unmercifully short shelf life. Village-wide outages happened frequently and unexpectedly, and could last a few hours or a week... there was no way to tell.

Compounding the problem, Mandalzuud's water supply - all concentrated in three main public wells - was brackish and visibly salty, like a poorly-stirred glass of powdered lemonade. Two of the wells were located disproportionately far from most homes, and it was many a villager who had to fuss over a mile-long walk to get the day's water. Herders let their livestock drink from these same locations, and so the ground surrounding the wells was perpetually littered with animal dung of all qualities.

There seemed to be no great concern about any of this.

Yet it was clear that the Mandalzuud of those days was in a state of perpetual judgment, forever existing under the threat of being swallowed by the Gobi. In the past few decades, the desert had been expanding, the grasses disappearing and the sandstorms worsening. Every year, the desert reclaimed another few tons of earth in its great tug of war with civilization. The local ponds and animal watering holes - which had served herders for generations – were drying up with alarming regularity, as the rocky sands of the Gobi crept closer and closer to Mandalzuud.

It was a place of bones... one of the thirstiest land-islands on the face of the Earth.

And I was stranded on it.

***

But in every place, no matter how austere, some people suffer less than others.

As for myself, I lived in the central district of town, in a newly-constructed ger near the village school. The ger was a modestly-sized but top-notch version, with head room enough to stand on a chair and barely touch the ceiling supports. The felt on the walls was fresh and warm, and the wooden door was solid (with a brawny deadbolt to boot), and I was surprised at how comfortable my new digs turned out to be.

The ger had its own yard and private outhouse (an almost ostentatious luxury in Mandalzuud), and it was hooked up directly to the main village power line with Peace Corps-certified electrical wiring. In the corner of the yard there was an oil drum for burning garbage, which was opposite a little wooden shack where the winter's coal and dung were stored. The wooden fence surrounding my yard was tall and comforting, and the gate was strong and sturdy... good for keeping out both wild dogs and wandering drunks.

Inside the ger, my furnishings were modest but comfort-able: a wooden frame and blanket mattress for a bed, a dry sink to wash in, an old desk and dresser from the school's dormitory, a thin, metal food shelf, and two, tiny-but-sturdy sitting stools. There was also a rusty-iron pot-belly stove, which had been lovingly restored for me by the village school's janitor. Near the stove, there was a metal bucket filled with dried dung chunks (the fuel de jour of the treeless Mandalzuud), a small bin of coal nuggets, and a stockpile of paper scraps for kindling. I strung up my Corps-issued mos-quito net around my bed - which as per tradition faced the north side of the ger - and hung up a rope clothesline near my dry sink where I draped my laundry.

My food shelf reflected the local cuisine of Mandalzuud. On the top shelf lay some farina instant wheat, ramen noo-dles, various teas, soup and spaghetti noodles, a stale loaf of bread, and a bottle of generic, canola cooking oil. Next to these things were my stockpiles of flour, salt, sugar and rice. On the shelf below, I had my cardboard boxes full of potatoes, onions and carrots (the only vegetables that would grow in the cursed Gobi terrain). I kept my perishables - butter, meat and the occasional bottle of goat milk – stored in a plastic cooler that I'd picked up in Ulaanbaatar.

And that was all of it.

In addition to my personal belongings and Corps gear, this was the sum total of my creature comforts in those days... the whole of my material wealth. But somehow, even this meager amount of possessions seemed like it was too much. When I visited the other villagers, I couldn't help but notice the vast amount of property that separated us. My neighbors didn't have electric water distillers. They didn't have pressurized fire extinguishers. They didn't have Tamiflu capsules, or private outhouses, or sometimes even electricity, for that matter.

But I did.

And in the end, despite all the deprivations and "hardships" I suffered those first few months in Mandalzuud, I was still the big shot from America with the hundred-dollar-a-month Peace Corps living allowance, which could have fed and clothed three, native Mongolians. I was still a big shot with a Corps-issued sleeping bag, a thousand-dollar guitar and emergency chlorine purification tablets. I was the big shot with a carbon monoxide detector, and a university degree and a Corps-issued rape whistle. And here I was, complaining about a few thousand beetles in my tent.

Some hero.

Some punishment.

***

Upon assignment to their permanent sites, the Peace Corps buys each volunteer one friend.

This friend is known as a "counterpart"... a combination peer/mentor in Corps parlance. These Corps subcontractors are tasked with taking their rookie volunteer under their wing and providing support services, much like Chimgee and Oyunn did during our training in Delgerkhovd.

The Corps does not pay them for their services... although counterparts are compensated in a number of other ways.

In keeping with Corps' tradition, counterparts are always longtime residents of the community. My own counterpart, a middle-aged woman named Tsetseg, was the resident foreign language teacher at the Mandalzuud school. She stood about 5' 6" - the average height for a Mongolian woman - and had a slight pot belly from eating nothing but meat and potatoes her whole life. She was only seven years older than me, but the Gobi ages people fiercely, and if you squinted, Tsetseg could have passed for my mother.

Her voice had an unmistakably positive energy to it, like the lady on the infomercial that tells you that "You *can* save a starving child, for only pennies a day."

She was born and raised in Mandalzuud, but was lucky enough to spend her teenage years at a public boarding school in the capitol city. Most teenagers fortunate enough to escape the Gobi never return, but Tsetseg was the exception, coming back to teach English in her old hometown when the Mongol government's official embracement of the language created a slew of ESL teaching jobs. And two years later, when the Peace Corps started to investigate Mandalzuud as a possible new volunteer site, my counterpart happened to be in the right place at the right time.

As the only fluent English speaker in the village, Tsetseg was the Corps' first and last choice for the position.

She was the one I went to when my power was shut off, or when there was a problem at the bank, or when I couldn't understand a change in my teaching schedule, or when any of the countless daily aggravations of Mongolian life left me in dire need of someone who could understand my words. She kept me informed, sane, centered and respected. She was the one responsible for getting me to a doctor if I got stabbed. She was the one who translated my gibberish to the others. She was my teacher. She was my student.

And in the end, she was my friend, above all else.

***

Besides Tsetseg, my in-country support system also included Khishigtuul and Purevdorj, a middle-aged wife and husband who lived in the *hashaa* next to mine. Much like my counterpart, they were part of my Corps-approved safety net, and like her, they didn't get compensated for their trouble. Nevertheless - perhaps because of the respect and glory that hosting an "American" would bring them... or perhaps simply because they were Good People - the two had pledged to help look after me in my first tremulous and vulnerable months in Mandalzuud.

Khishigtuul was the village school's director and my immediate supervisor, the Mongolian equivalent of a school principal. She was a big, jolly lady with generous cheekbones, who took her role as matronly guardian of the American seriously. She loved to bring over weird little dishes that "an American should try" - barbecued marmot, homemade goat-yogurt, horse rump with rice - and was always scolding me for eating too much *kaash*... the Mongolian version of cream of wheat.

"Kaash is for Mongolian *babies!*" she would tell me, looking down at me and clicking her tongue with disapproval as I ate yet another pot of farina.

"I'm young at heart," I would tell her, feasting on my gruel.

Her husband, Purevdorj, a broad-shouldered and friendly man, was the village's resident global businessman. He had spent a little time in several countries (including the United States), and was fiercely proud of his business card collection. He had also acquired a fervent fascination with James Bond somewhere along the line, and had seen more Bond flicks than I had previously known existed.

Purevdorj was determined to work on his English while I was in Mongolia, and whenever he came over to visit, he would speak in English and I would reply in Mongolian. It didn't really work out most of the time, but I appreciated the attempt, and I was always glad to have *yet another* dialogue about how the weather was or what kinds of foods we liked.

Together, Khishigtuul and Purevdorj provided a comforting resource next door, and neither one ever spoke a single angry word to me.

Two of the Good People, if ever such a thing existed.

***

Khishigtuul had placed me in charge of teaching ESL to the 4th and 5th grades... my official "foot in the door" and reason for being in Mandalzuud.

The Mandalzuud Soum Eight-Year School was located in a run down, Soviet-style building, which had been built way back during the great U.S.S.R.-led infrastructure expansion in the 1950s. Three hundred students crammed themselves into six disintegrating classrooms every day, each with haunted-looking windows, nightmarish temperature swings and weird smells that couldn't be bleached away. The school was too small to fit the entire student population at one time, so they rotated in shifts; the older students would go to class in the mornings and the younger students would replace them in the afternoons. Only two of the classrooms had electricity, and every surface in the school was scarred, as if the building had caught smallpox and barely survived.

During those first few weeks of teaching, my head was filled with all of the dreams that the iconic American teacher films had taught me... the troubled inner-city kid who is secretly a musical savant... the unconventional educator who inspires his hopelessly conformist students... the troubled-but-talented teacher who is saved by his students' faith and joy... all of it... the glory... the redemption... the molding of young minds and souls. I was going to be Robin Williams in Dead Poet's Society. I was going to be Morgan Freeman from Lean on Me. Hell, I was going to be Michelle Pheiffer from Dangerous Minds.

It was almost a month, before I figured out that nobody in the entire school gave a shit about learning English, and my presence at school was almost entirely ceremonial.

The Hood Ornament returns.

Ah, Hollywood. Do things *ever* work out the way that you promise they will?

But perhaps it was good that those early days in Mandalzuud were too busy for me to fully reflect on any "deeper meaning" behind it all. There were too many places to remember, people to meet, customs to learn. After all, when choking in the winds of a sandstorm, one seldom stops to write poetry. And all too soon, I would learn that existence in the Gobi was much different than the lushness I had come to know in Delgerkhovd, with its sparkling river and pastoral mountains and wild marijuana fields.

This was a different Mongolia, altogether. It was harder. It was sadder.

And I had a lot of catching up to do on both fronts.

~ 10 ~

The Jesus Dentists

On the third day of October, Jesus arrived in Mandalzuud.

Or rather, he sent his messengers, Howard Younger and Don Scruggs ... a pair of American dentists from Miami and Colorado. The two had been recruited by Global Concern - one of the largest, Christian nonprofit missions in America - as part of the organization's effort to provide free dental services to rural Mongolia (and subsequently win the hearts and souls of the natives). Now, after two weeks of traveling through the Mongolian southeast plains, doling out their much-needed services along the way, Younger and Scruggs were coming to our tiny village of Mandalzuud... and they were packing redemption in heavy quantities.

My inquisitive hashaa neighbor, Purevdorj, had been placed in charge of arranging sleeping quarters for the Jesus Dentists and their entourage during their two-day stop in Mandalzuud. In his haste to do a good deed, he had taken the liberty of telling Scruggs and Young that I would stop by the village clinic for a visit the following day, an invitation that I reluctantly accepted only because I didn't know how to turn it down.

They sounded exactly like the type of fuckers that I had trekked six thousand miles to escape. But Purevdorj was bursting at the seams that we should meet because we were "Americans, all Americans", and eventually, he wore me down with his exuberance.

"Friends... America," Purevdorj insisted in his broken English, giving me the thumbs-up signal. "Tomorrow... One 'o' clock."

"They're not really my *friends*," I tried to tell him, but he wasn't listening.

"Tomorrow," he repeated, smiling at me and turning his back. "One 'o' clock."

And that's how the next afternoon, I found myself trudging down to the Mandalzuud health clinic to meet a pair of goddamn dentists.

***

Word of the Jesus Dentists' arrival had spread quickly among the villagers.

When I arrived, Mongolians were spilling out the front doors like Styrofoam pellets from a hemorrhaging beanbag chair. Inside, the clinic's tiny waiting room was packed full of villagers, all of whom were splayed out over the floor and against the walls, trying to outdo each other with exaggerated groans and grimaces in the hopes of getting one of the day's precious dental appointments. I recognized some of them from the village, but many of the others were from the khuudo, herders whom seldom came to town and had not been to a dentist in years, if not decades. For some, the daily pain in their jaws had become routine, one more sad little bit of daily suffering that was neither to be condemned nor regretted. I knew that if they didn't get a chance to see the Jesus dentists – and many would not - most of the herders would simply opt to rip their own teeth out at home.

Briefly glancing around the waiting room, I saw that it was festooned with Christian propaganda flyers and pamphlets, the same sort of stuff that you see in subway stations and AA meetings. I wandered over to an end table near the clinic entrance and picked one up.

"Jesus Saves!" the little pulp booklet proclaimed in English, with no Mongolian translation.

Grimacing, I placed it back on the table.

Navigating my way through the minefield of villagers, I made my way to the front of the waiting room. As I did, a nurse that I recognized from one of the adult English classes that I'd been teaching walked past, a chart in one hand and a dental mirror in the other.

"Chimgee!" I called out, holding out my hand like I was hailing a cab.

"Eric! Hello! What are you doing here?" a grinning Chimgee asked me in Mongolian.

I told her that I was here to meet the dentists.

"They are working with patients now," she told me, pointing to a closed door beyond the hallway. "The last children of the day. Oh yes, we are very, very busy today."

"Ah," I said, nodding. "What time should I return?"

"Oh," Chimgee said, "You don't have to wait. There is the door. Go in."

"Now?" I asked, surprised. "But they're with patients... I can wait until they're finished... and don't I have to go wash my hands or at least knock the shit off my boots or something?"

"Zuger," she chastised, waving for me to follow. With the crowded waiting room of Mongolians eyeing me in a polite-hostile way - *Why does the rich American get to cut in line?* - Chimgee led me down the hall and let me into the operating room.

"Please speak quietly," she said and left me to it, shutting the door behind her.

And just like that, I was standing before The Lord's representatives.

As I had anticipated, it was terrible... like being stuck in church on a hot, summer's day. Although it was October and breezy, the windowless examination room had zero circulation, and there was a sticky heat in the air that matted the hair on my neck within seconds. In the corner, a small electric drilling and suction machine hummed and filled the room with white noise. The rest of the Jesus Dentists' gear was stored in plastic fishing tackle boxes, which were stacked all around us in disorganized heaps.

My gaze snapped to the center of the room, to the bizarre orgy of dentistry on display before me. The group hadn't noticed my presence yet, so I quietly watched them for a moment as they toiled and suffered together. There

– in huge, monstrous, frontal profile - the Jesus Dentists were perched on stools, hard at work with their terrifying implements of destruction. The one on the left was about sixty years old, with close-cropped silver hair and a military posture. The one on the right – about forty years and three hundred pounds – breathed so loudly that I could hear him under his face mask. Two grubby, young khuudo children lay terrified before them in a pair of medical cots, their mothers standing nearby to help keep the squirming to a minimum. Next to them, a young, urban Mongolian woman in khakis and a button-down shirt stood, translating commands and questions back and forth.

I cleared my throat and the entire room turned to look over in my direction.

"Hi," I said, holding my hand up meekly, suddenly wishing that I hadn't come at all. "Eric Kiefer. You must be the Jesus Dentists."

"Ahhh yessss..... they do call us that, don't they?" replied the silver-haired dentist on the left, nodding hello. His voice was half-muffled from the paper surgical mask on his face, and when he spoke, he sounded eerily like Batman. "You must be the Peace Corps worker. It's a pleasure to meet you. Name's Howard Younger... Purevdorj said that you might be stopping by. You'll understand if I don't get up to shake your hand."

He gestured at the rotund dentist on his right. "This is my compatriot, the esteemed Dr. Scruggs."

Scruggs nodded at me, drill in hand, eyes blinking with hunger and fatigue. "Pleasure."

Younger nodded towards the Mongolian woman beside him. "And this lady over here is Enhkbat, our translator. I'd introduce our patients and their mothers – you see them standing right there – but I think they have other things on their minds right now."

Unaware of the context of our conversation, the children continued to lie on their backs, their suffocating fish mouths wide open with fear, wondering what the hell the village English teacher was doing here.

"I can come back later..." I said, gesturing at the kids and taking a step backwards.

"No, no, don't worry, this is the easiest work we've done all day... fillings only," Younger insisted. He glanced back down at his patient's mouth, still agape with fear. "We were about to break for lunch after we're done with these two kids, in fact. Why don't you hang around for a few minutes, then come back and have some spaghetti with us."

"Spaghetti?" I asked.

Scruggs nodded. "Spaghetti."

"Spaghetti," I confirmed.

So not knowing what else to do, I stood around uncomfortably and watched the Jesus Dentists turn back to their patients. It was a strange process. Lacking a road-worthy alternative, the dentists had been forced to pack their medical supplies in a series of fishing tackle boxes. As they withdrew their instruments of pain from the tackle boxes, and bent over their victim's mouths like expert anglers, I couldn't help but wonder what it felt like to be a hooked trout. After five minutes or so, both dentists called it quits and released their patients, who went scurrying out of the clinic as fast as their feet could take them. Their mothers lingered behind a minute to thank the dentists (and to give me a funny look), then they slowly followed their wailing children out of the operating room, letting the door slam behind them.

"Ahhhhh, another couple of souls saved," Younger said when they were gone, standing up and taking off his mask and latex gloves. The others followed his lead.

"Enhkbat, would you tell everyone waiting outside that we're going to lunch?"

She nodded and set off down the hall. As the translator veered off for the waiting room to break the bad news, we all walked down the hallway to the clinic's kitchen/staff room. When we got there, a small Mongolian man with a lopsided mustache was sitting and reading a newspaper, occasionally stirring a simmering pot on a small hotplate.

"Eric, meet Chohka, our driver," said Scruggs, walking over to the dry sink to wash his hands. "In addition to being a top-notch tour guide, mechanic and chauffer, Chohka here is also quite a cook. Makes a great middle-of-the-Gobi spaghetti. Plus, he even speaks English. Chohka, this is Eric... he's a Peace Corps volunteer here in Mandalzuud. He's teaching English... right?"

"Right," I said, shaking Chohka's hand, slightly embarrassed by the banality of my assignment.

Chohka looked up at me and nodded solemnly, unimpressed, but polite enough to fake like he was.

Meanwhile, Scruggs had been staring at the pot of spaghetti like Emperor Nero eyeing a book of matches, and finally the portly dentist could take no more.

"Is the food ready?" he asked, taking his turn at the dry sink.

Chohka nodded.

"Then let's eat!" Scruggs declared happily, scrubbing his hands.

And so the feast was on.

***

As we all sat down at a small folding table, Chohka ladled us all out heaping bowls of noodles and red sauce. After another minute, Enkhbat emerged from the waiting room and joined us. Then, as we gathered at our places, Younger led us in a prayer and we all dug into the spaghetti.

It was delicious, Jesus or no Jesus.

"Where did you get tomatoes?" I asked, smacking my lips in appreciation as I chewed. "I haven't seen a tomato since I've been in Mongolia."

Younger twirled spaghetti onto his fork. "From Ulaanbaatar, where else? We arrived in the city two weeks ago, met our Global Concern contacts, and headed out on tour two days later. Since then we've been travelling up through the Gobi in a loop. We'll keep going until we make our way back to U.B."

"How many villages have you been to so far?" I asked.

Scruggs held up nine chubby – yet surprisingly dexterous - fingers.

"And two more before we head back to Ulaanbaatar," added Younger, jabbing with his fork. "Then two new dentists from Global Concern will come in and take our place in the spring. We've got a pool back in the States that's been rotating for a couple of years, now. In fact, this is my fifth tour... I think that it's Don's... what... your third go 'round?"

Scruggs held up four fingers as he continued chewing a huge forkful of spaghetti.

"Global Concern makes it easy," Younger continued. "Our routes are pre-calculated, our contacts are prearranged, our vehicle is rented and outfitted, our meals are cooked..."

As Younger carried on, I thought about the vast amounts of taxpayer money that it took to train and send me – one lousy Peace Corps volunteer – out into the Gobi. Then I thought about the amount of cash that it would take to sponsor these dentists and their entire weird caravan of drills and propaganda.

And it didn't add up.

"... and best of all, we don't have to wade through the endless piles of paperwork that it would normally take to get two, well-meaning American doctors over the Mongolian border..." continued Younger.

"Man, Global Concern must be pretty loaded these days to be able to send you all out pro bono like this," I interrupted abruptly. "I hope that you're saving receipts."

The Jesus Dentists laughed.

"Would it surprise you to hear that Don and I pay our own way while we're here?" Younger asked. "Global Concern's main role is to *organize*, not to *donate*. Did you see all those drills and suction machines and gauze and needles and pain killers? Well, Global Concern helped us pick them up from a Mongolian medical supply company. They made the arrangements for their delivery, and even filled out the transport forms for us. But in the end, it's never been Global Concern that has been signing on the dotted line when the bill comes... it's been me and Don. Now I don't mean to make it sound bigger than it is, but this trip probably cost me about $10,000 – out of my own pocket – and I'm sure that it's about the same for my partner here."

"But what's a few thousand bucks, compared to this amazing opportunity to heal the world?" added Scruggs instantly.

Younger nodded in agreement. "It's about healing the world... healing the world."

With a mouth full of spaghetti, I looked across the table at the Jesus Dentists. Their hands were calm, their faces serene, their eyes unwavering and their auras honest. And suddenly, feeling like a troglodyte and an arsehole, I began to think that maybe these people weren't all that bad after all. I had come expecting the missionaries who destroyed Montezuma and slaughtered Metacom, but from what I could tell, these two were simply a couple of old dentists looking for their golden tickets into heaven, a pair of believers who in fact, had done a lot more concrete "good" for Mongolia than I had... on their own dime for that matter.

And the truth was, "healing the world" sounded a whole lot like "saving" it... maybe even better.

Younger must have noticed that there was an internal dialogue taking place in my head. "Look," he said. "Before you get the wrong idea, we didn't exactly have to break the bank and sell the farm to buy our tickets out here. Dentists make a comfortable living in America, and it was either come to Mongolia this year or vacation in the Bahamas. I don't think that any of us are fooled into thinking that we're martyrs, or anything like that. In fact, doing this reminds me of exactly how privileged I am, and how much of the world's suffering I've been spared."

Younger paused in thought for a moment. "Enkhbat, what was that village we were in two weeks ago?"

"*Deren soum*," the translator replied.

"Yeah... Deren. We had this one gentleman, a goat herder if I'm not mistaken, wait *five days* for us to arrive. Five, long, pain-racked days. When we finally got to town, his tooth was rotten clear to the root... black as tar. But did he complain? Did he curse the Lord's name? Not for a moment. I tell you, Job has nothing on someone who hasn't seen a dentist for twenty years."

"If you've got villagers waiting a week for you," I said, "there must be a hell of a waiting list. How do you see all of them?"

Scruggs laughed, sending flecks of red sauce leaping from his mouth. "*All* of them? That's impossible. You saw those villagers in the waiting room. That line won't shrink an inch until we've left the village. It spills outside of the building, like they're waiting on line for sold-out concert tickets. It's like this everywhere... abcessed gums, exposed tooth roots, chipped and broken incisors, eroded enamel, periodontitis, molar erosion and cracking... I've stopped counting how many teeth I yanked long ago."

"Then how do you decide who to see?" I asked.

Upon hearing my question, Younger looked over at Scruggs, exchanging something unspoken. The two conversed for a moment in their minds, and I was obviously not invited. It was a strange reaction, and I noticed that my question had plucked a hidden tension in the room, as if I had struck a sour note on an invisible guitar string.

"Well," Younger finally said, glancing over at his colleague for confirmation, "we see children first as a general rule.

Scruggs nodded in agreement.

"If we have time after that – like today - we try to reward the ones that have been saved."

"Saved?" I asked.

"Meaning that they accept Jesus as their Lord and Savior."

I looked from one face to another, seeing the same earnestness that had impressed me before. And then in one fell moment, it all added up... they were only treating Mongolians who said that they were Christian.

"But what about the ones that won't... um... accept Jesus?" I asked.

"Salvation is much more important than dental care," Scruggs told me, meeting my eyes with an abrupt and zealous conviction.

"Oh," I said, unaware of how to reply.

Younger nodded. "You've got to understand that we're spreading the Gospel through dental care. That's our main goal here in Mongolia. We were sent by the Lord. After all, what's the suffering of someone with an abscessed root, compared to the eternal suffering of a soul in hell or purgatory? Jesus can't heal those who don't believe in him…"

And I nodded desolately as they continued.

I finished my spaghetti with a hasty sadness, listening patiently as the two persisted to talk fire and brimstone. The moment they finished, I dropped my fork into my plate and said that I had to leave.

No, no… you didn't say anything to offend me. Really, I was raised Christian myself… I can say the "Hail Mary" and everything! The spaghetti was absolutely delicious, by the way… my hat is off to you, Chohka. Anyway, I appreciate that you let me hang around while you worked, and everything. It was definitely a learning experience, to say the least. But I've got to finish up my lesson plans for tomorrow – my students have this huge test on the present continuous tense – and I should probably be going. If you get a free moment before you leave, definitely come to say hello… my ger is easy to find, just ask for "The American"…

The Jesus Dentists looked disappointed, but Younger said that it was about time they got back to work anyway. I went around the room and shook everyone's hands, and we all made a big ceremony out of exchanging email addresses.

And that's how we left it.

As I left the clinic, Chohka's spaghetti weighed heavy in my gut, slowing my steps to a fatigued plod. I thought about the Jesus Dentists as I shuffled back to my ger, a looming sadness engulfing me in its gluttonous arms. These people had spent thousands of their own dollars to come to Mongolia, traveled around the Gobi in a shit-heap van for weeks, spent ten-hour days slaving away for no pay, and endured unknown hardship upon hardship. They had liberated dozens of children and adults from debilitating pain, eased the suffering of hundreds more, and even cooked a wayward Peace Corps volunteer a spaghetti dinner.

But they wouldn't save you if you didn't believe in Jesus.

Outside, the wind had graduated from a gust to a gale, and the sun was a rotten peach in the sky that diminished in hue with each passing minute. A sudden breeze reminded me of my need to get back indoors, and I quickened my pace through the village. The weather had been steadily changing for weeks, undergoing a rapid and foreboding metamorphosis, and although winter wouldn't arrive for weeks yet, there was no doubt that the motherfucker had received its invitation and had sent an early RSVP.

But all the way home, a single, dreadful thought kept running through my mind, and no matter how fast I tried to move my legs, the awful notion doggedly pursued. It followed me through my dreams that night, nipping and lapping at my heels as I tried to outpace its mournful ululations. And all through the coming winter, through all the death and sickness and sadness and self-realization that followed, I would never fail to cringe in fear at remembering...

If these truly helpful people carry this sick truth at the heart of their humanitarianism, what terrors lie dormant in my own soul?

~ 11 ~

Wintering in the Bad Places

On November 3, it was warm enough to rain.

This would not happen again for almost four months.

The winters of the Gobi Desert are legendary, arriving abruptly in early November and coming on severe. During this time, there is no rain... only snow and ice. Winter temperatures can drop to forty degrees below Celsius - lower if you count wind chill - cold enough to turn a puddle of piss into a beetle ice-skating rink within an hour. Mongolian winters can freeze a jug of water solid overnight, kill a herd of cattle in a week and ruin an entire potato harvest in a month. In this kind of absolute environment, everything without fur or fire dies.

The more exposed settlements of the Mongolian Gobi are especially prone to massive and mortal cold snaps. These are called *Zuud* winters, and are not spoken of until they happen.

In the worst Zuuds, there are dead bodies everywhere.

***

My first Mongol winter began innocently enough.

As the equinox drew closer, light snows began to fall, powdery and gossamer stuff that the wind would blow away in spiraling, psychedelic trails. I'd go outside during the day - all bundled up in my U.S. Postal Service surplus winter coat - and watch the swirls of snow and dust ripple against each other like a fog, as if I was strolling on the surface of Jupiter. At night, my evening fires would melt the frost from atop my ger, making droplets of ice water leak through and fall on the stove... little universe dollops that evaporated instantly with thrilling sizzles and puffs. For a while, at least, the Mongolian winter was beautiful.

But that all changed one morning in late November, when I woke up and saw my frozen breath in the air.

From that day on, the cold was no longer quaint or rustic. It was creeping death. At night, Mandalzuud's stray dogs curled up in the dying grasses and howled to each other, moaning for pity in a secret language that I would never understand. The herders began to wrap their cattle in old blankets to keep them alive, and as the summertime watering holes began to ice over, their cows would roam the outskirts of the village with a zombie-like, relentless thirst, lapping at any snow on the ground that hadn't turned to permafrost.

The felt walls of my ger kept the worst of the cold out... as long as there was a fire in the stove. But the second that fire died, a bone-blasting chill began to permeate my world, which drooped around in the air like a phantom until I lit another blaze and chased it away. My evening fire began to be kindled earlier and earlier... first at eight 'o' clock, then seven, then six. Soon, I was lighting fires as soon as I got home from school in the afternoon.

Soon, I was going to sleep when the fire went out.

The Corps had placed Purevdorj and Khishigtuul in charge of keeping me stocked with coal and dung, providing them with a monthly stipend to pay for the cost. They kept this fuel heaped in a tiny shed in the corner of the hashaa. I was a little nervous because the shed had no lock, but Purevdorj told me not to worry about such things.

"But what if someone steals from me?" I asked him one day, after he had helped me to move in a fresh pile of dung.

"No...no," he told me in English, looking at me like I was insane. It was unthinkable that a person would steal coal or dung from a neighbor... it would have been like someone stealing a crucifix from a church, or thieving baseball cards from a Make-A-Wish kid.

"Trust... trust," Purevdorj told me.

"Sure... Trust," I said, thinking about the look on my host father's face, on that long-ago night in Delgerkhovd.

***

By the time December rolled around, getting my weekly water supply from the well had evolved from an unpleasant chore into a bona-fide hazard.

The closest well was a two-cigarette walk across a morass of sand, and for a person with an unwieldy handcart and a mammoth jug of water, the need for water was a cruel master. And all through that winter, pushing my goddamn water cart through the desert on a freezing winter's after-noon, it felt like I was the Sisyphus of the Gobi, rolling my punishment boulder up the hills of Hell.

Even with gloves on, the gnawing December winds would stiffen and numb my fingers, and holding the frozen and frayed well rope felt like grasping an icy umbilical cord in my bare hands. Folded in half, I'd slop freezing water all over myself, wrenching my back as I hefted the well bucket into the light of the Mongolian afternoon. I would return home from my task in a foul, exhausted mood, fully aware that this wasn't even considered a daunting task to a Mongolian... in fact, it was typically a child's job.

I was reminded of this humbling truth one frigid day at the well, when I ran into one of my fifth grade students, a particularly snotty little fucker named Khoonbish. The boy almost never bathed, spent most of his time picking on the unpopular students, and had almost no natural aptitudes other than sensing weakness. Despite this, I never hit him... although many of the other teachers at school had.

The boy's water jugs were almost full as I came upon him at the well, huffing and blowing snot all over himself, yank-ing hand over hand on the rope of the water pail. I noticed that he wasn't wearing gloves, and his tattered winter coat was already half-soaked with well water and sweat.

"Yo," I said as I approached the well, holding up my hand.

Khoonbish looked at me for a long second, then turned back to the well and continued to haul water.

"Good to see you too, you little fink," I muttered in English, just loud enough for him to hear if he tried. I hung around until his last jug was full, then as he finished, I sidled up next to him with my own jug and laid it down next to the well. I closed my eyes and turned to stretch my back.

When I turned around, Khoonbish had my jug in his hand and was kneeling over the well, about to start hauling water.

I was shocked.

"Hey kid," I said, tapping him on the back. "I can do that... *Bi chattan. Zuger.*"

He ignored me and continued to lower the bucket into the well.

I stood around helplessly, not sure what to say but suddenly guilty. "I mean, thanks... but don't worry about it. Really. I can haul my own water. Cease. Desist. *Zogsoch!*"

And Khoonbish did stop then, spinning around with a puzzled look on his face.

"*Yarcen ve?*" he asked me, truly perplexed as to why I had asked him to stop.

I stood there looking at Khoonbish, his ungloved hands red and chapped, his scrawny coat doused with icy water, exhausted and still a half-mile from his ger. *Why would this little punk be so keen to help me*, I wondered.

Khoonbish continued to stare at me, rope in hand.

He must be trying to earn a little money, I suddenly realized, shaking my head at myself for being so dumb. I checked my pocket to make sure I had some bills, then gestured for Khoonbish to continue.

He turned back to the well, muttering something derogatory under his breath.

As Khoonbish worked, I leaned back against my water cart and lit a cigarette. *Might as well get my money's worth*, I thought. But whenever the wind picked up enough to make me shiver, I would glance down at Khoonbish, feeling a pang of guilt for letting this poor kid slave away in the freezing weather while I stood around foppishly, like an nineteenth century aristocrat observing a child chimney sweep at work.

But the kid never wavered and never looked back, and after ten minutes of hard work, he had filled my jug completely to the top. Exhausted, he handed my jug back, not saying a word or even making eye contact.

"Not a bad job kid," I said, reaching into my pocket to take out a couple hundred turgrugs. As I did, I saw Khoonbish start to walk away.

"*Hoy!*" I called out after him, taking the bills and waving them in the air. "*Bedgie!*"

Khoonbish stopped in his tracks.

"*Meh*," I shouted. "You forgot your money, kid!"

The boy turned back for a moment, staring at me with the same perplexed look that he had when I first asked him to stop hauling water.

"*Meh*," I repeated, holding out the dough.

For one instant, his dirty little face contracted, the muscles in his cheeks twitching involuntarily. But his brief flash of greed was over quickly, and a second later, the boy shook his head at me in refusal.

"*Zuger bagsha*," he said, declining my offering.

And with that, the khuudo rat hefted up the handlebars of his pitiful little water cart and left me standing there, a fistful of money in my hand and a full jug of icy water at my feet.

The value of one good deed, indeed.

***

In January, I got two new neighbors... Purevdorj's elderly parents, Ravjah and Khulaan.

They were both khuudo-raised, old school Mongols, true creatures of the desert, about seventy years old and worn to wrinkles by years of ger living. But despite the pair's resilience, it seemed that age had finally caught up to Ravjah, and as his father slowly grew more infirm, my neighbor gradually realized that his parents wouldn't be able to last the winter on their own. At that point, it was agreed that coming back to Mandalzuud would be in the best interest of everyone.

Lo and behold, a few weeks later, there was a new "temporary" ger erected in the far corner of my hashaa.

I should have known that company was inevitable. After all, I was "The American"... with his nearly empty hashaa for one... his free supply of dung and coal... his easy-to-splice hookup to the power grid... his need to be watched over, day and night... his need for responsibility and purpose.

And it was time that I started earning my keep.

When I first met him, Ravjah was already thin and sick, healthy enough to grasp a hammer but not to use it, which was sad, because the old man's calloused hands spoke of years of manual labor. He was forever coughing – loud,

hacking spasms that I could hear all the way from my ger
- and he spent most of his time in bed, watching the Mongolian National Broadcast station on a tiny, black and white
television.

It was clear from the beginning that the old man hated
my guts.

The stinker was pleasant enough to me whenever his son
was around, but whenever our paths crossed in private, the
old man would only sneer at me and cough phlegm into his
handkerchief. I figured that Ravjah would warm to me after
a little while, but the time never came, and he continued
to shoot me bitter looks whenever our paths would cross.
Whenever I tried to visit his ger, I was reluctantly allowed
in – the Mongol rules of conduct requiring him to allow me
entrance - but I was utterly ignored until I left, as if I was
a mosquito that had found its way inside and might find
its way out again, given enough time. Eventually I gave up
trying to talk to the old coot at all, and the time soon came
when I was avoiding him altogether.

His wife, Khulaan, was a different matter.

She was a short and stocky woman, who moved with a bit
of a stoop and a curve to her back, like a desert turtle on two
legs. Every time I saw her, she was puffing on a humungous,
conical, hand-rolled cigarette, which would droop from the
corner of her mouth like a huge, white wart. In public, Khulaan followed the lead of her husband and shunned me, but I
could tell that she secretly liked me, because every now and
then she would bring me over some leftover *bohdz*, or some
meat cakes that she claimed "were just lying around."

In return for her kindness, I would occasionally offer to fill up her water jug because I "just happened to be going to the well." It was an arrangement that worked fine, making us both feel as if we were being surreptitiously clever and charitable at the same time.

But when Ravjah discovered our little scheme, he didn't take the news well.

For weeks after he learned of our barter program, the old man insisted on attempting to struggle to the well for himself, despite the ardent admonishing of his wife and son. Every morning it would be a big ordeal - Ravjah spending about an hour bundling up in his winter del while Khulaan chided him and tried to force him back into bed - an ordeal which would always end with Ravjah outside, feebly struggling out the hashaa door with the water cart, wheezing and sputtering his way to the well like a dying ox on his last plow.

Sometimes he would almost make it to the well before he ran out of energy, but more often than not, Ravjah would return empty handed and deathly sick, his mission grinding to a disheartening failure a dozen steps outside the hashaa gate. Eventually the old man became too sick to even make it out the hashaa gate anymore, and the saddening farce stopped being played out. But every now and then - just when you thought that he was done for good – the old bastard would emerge from his ger, gaunt as an anorexic lark in his winter *del,* a grim look of determination steeling his wizened face.

And he would try it all over again.

***

While fetching water one morning a few weeks after my new neighbors arrived, I made it halfway to the well before I noticed that the water cart's left tire was flat... flat as an apple decomposed beyond revival... flat as a cock trapped in an iron maiden.

I immediately knew the cause... Ravjah's latest water gathering attempt.

With a sigh, I dragged the cart back to our hashaa and returned it to its usual place behind the coal shed. I went next door, hoping to tell Purevdorj or Khishigtuul about the tire so they could help me find someone to patch it up. But nobody answered when I knocked, so I went and borrowed the school's water cart, meaning to tell Purevdorj about the tire later in the evening. Returning home exhausted, I forgot all about the flat tire until about six 'o' clock, when I heard a knock at my ger door.

I swung it open to find a fuming Ravjah, his craggy hands high on his bony hips, his forehead wrinkled with the consternation of someone who has just spent eight hours at the DMV.

"Can I help you?" I asked in Mongolian.

"*What happened to the water cart?*" he demanded in a heavily accented slur. The words tumbled from the old man's frail mouth like concrete from the back of a mixer, and it took all my concentration to understand what he was saying.

"Oh yeah... the water cart," I said at last. "That thing is broken, man... *ajilakhgui.*"

I nodded for emphasis and gave the old man my friendliest forced smile, certain that the conversation was over. But he continued to stand in the doorway, shaking his head, a strange look of animosity on his face.

"What happened?" he demanded impatiently, pointing outside. *"What happened to the water cart?"*

I shrugged. I didn't quite understand what the problem was. It was a flat tire... case closed. But as I stood there dumbly in the doorway, Ravjah staring me down with a cross glare, I realized that there was a challenge behind the old man's words, something accusatory yet defensive, like an old man in line at the supermarket getting ready to argue with the cashier about coupons that he knows are expired.

It was then that I realized Ravjah was blaming *me* for popping the tire.

"Bish-ay, bish-ay," I said quickly, stuttering with my clumsy Mongolian. "You don't understand. I didn't do this. It wasn't me."

"Then who?" Ravjah hissed caustically, pointing a crooked finger in my direction.

"I don't know," I insisted. "I wanted to get water, but the tire was flat. I didn't see. I don't know."

After hearing my excuse, the old man began coughing in immediate indignation. His hacking wheeze sounded terrible, and instinctively I started towards him to see if he was alright, but Ravjah waved curtly for me to stop in my tracks.

"It was you," he accused, clearing his throat of phlegm and breathing through his mouth. He took his crummy handkerchief out of his pocket and spat into it. *"I know it was*

you. And now you are lying. You lie to an old man. You should be ashamed..."

"OH YEAH?" I interrupted. The bastard's accusations had set off my fight or flight response, and before I could stop myself, I found myself snapping back at him in English, fully aware that he wouldn't understand a word I was saying.

"Well, maybe you broke the cart, you despicable old fuck! Maybe you're the liar! I don't need this shit... I'm a goddamn U.S. Peace Corps volunteer... and I came here to save *you* goddamn it... don't you realize that... I came here to save YOU!"

And as soon as the words came out of my mouth, I knew that I had crossed the line.

Although Ravjah didn't understand a word that I had said, the context of my response was clear enough. The old man made an inhaling hissing noise, the Mongolian way of saying that I was full of bullshit. Then he immediately turned away, marched back to his ger and shut the door behind him, leaving me standing there in the threshold feeling terrible.

And that was the end of it.

In the next weeks, through begrudged mutual timing, Ravjah and I managed to accidentally bump into each other as little as possible, like grumpy old farts forced to coexist in the same apartment complex. I was left with no remedy for what I had said, but I knew that what happened couldn't be apologized for anyway, only forgotten. And as an American in the Gobi, there were so many other things to haunt myself with, I soon managed to forget all about the crazy, old man next door.

We once again became strangers.

And then, one frigid Thursday in late January - just when I had gotten used to our arrangement - Purevdorj came to my ger and told me that the old coot was dying.

***

"Dying?" I asked.

Purevdorj nodded sadly, and told me that a monk from Mandalgobi would be visiting as soon as possible to perform the traditional Mongol death rites. In an apologetic voice, he asked me to stay as far away as possible from Ravjah's ger when the death lama arrived.

"These ceremonies are for family only," he said in Mongolian. "And although you are almost like family – and sometimes more than that - some things must remain secrets. Do you understand?"

I promised him that I wouldn't intrude.

The death lama arrived at our hashaa three days later. Remembering my promise to Purevdorj, I kept far away from the ceremonies. But try as I might, the whole scene was impossible to completely ignore. All through the day I could hear the monk chanting, banging on a ceremonial hand drum and calling out to the heavens in his mysterious, old Mongol dialect. When I went outside for a cigarette, I would smell musky incense wafting from Ravjah's ger, thick and odiferous, like something a mortician would use to mask the smell of a decaying body.

And I waited.

Two days after the death lama's arrival, Purevdorj came over to tell me that the monk had begun performing his last rites.

"It will all be over soon," he promised in a low voice, speaking in Mongolian.

"No problem," I told him. "Some things, you just can't rush."

***

The next day, I saw Ravjah for the last time.

I had stepped outside for a cigarette and was quietly leaning against my door, when the old man emerged from his death ger, supported on Purevdorj's arm, shivering and shaking with each step. His skin was pale and waxy, his pace slow and gasping, his head wobbly as a newborn.

But he was still alive.

Purevdorj was in a deep concentration, focused on holding his father steady while simultaneously trying to fool the old man into thinking that he was walking on his own. For his part, Ravjah seemed to buy into the illusion. His eyes were focused intently on a spirit world that nobody could see, blazing with the dim intensity of a spent light bulb in its last flickering seconds of malfunction. Together, the father and son made their way towards the outhouse... and I realized that Ravjah was about to have his last dignified bowel movement.

I quietly watched them from my ger, saying nothing.

As the pair made their way across the hashaa yard, a cloud that had been covering the sky suddenly split open, spilling a burst of sunlight on the old man's ghoulish face. Ravjah mumbled something to his son, and the two stopped for a moment. For what was seconds to us - but surely seemed like eternities to him - the old man lingered in the sun's warmth, like a death row prisoner on his last walk to the electric chair.

And I knew that he was at peace.

But at last, the moment passed, and the old man opened his eyes. His back dropped out from under him... he clutched his son for support... and the two recommenced their mummy shamble to the outhouse. As they did, the old man swung his head in my direction. By pure coincidence, for a brief moment - no longer than a single beat of a shit-fly's wings - our eyes met.

And that was all it took.

As soon as he saw me, Ravjah's spine instantly straightened, as if infused with a titanium rod. Stopping dead in his tracks, Ravjah raised his bony finger at me, as if he was the Grim Reaper identifying his next charge.

"The water cart..." Ravjah croaked in old Mongolian, his gravelly voice filled with phlegm and vaguely recollected anger. *"What happened to the water cart?"*

Purevdorj, stopped in his tracks by his father's unexpected outburst, raised an eyebrow at me in surprise.

"I don't know..." I muttered weakly, not sure what to say, looking to Purevdorj and pleading silently for help. My neighbor tried to pick his father back up and aim him back towards the outhouse, but the old man would have none of it, twisting out of his son's grasp with a delirious nimbleness that surprised us both.

"*YOU DID THIS!*" he hollered at me in Mongolian, putting every last ounce of inner strength and focus into the words, infusing them with the raw power of a dozen atom bombs. His words were strong and clear, released by the honest tongue of a dying man. As Ravjah hollered, his eyes bulged and his legs wobbled, and his eyes began to roll up in his head. I saw his fists clench tighter... tighter... tighter... and I knew that the old bastard was about to make himself pass out.

"*YOU DID ALL OF THIS!*" Ravjah cried, his spidery veins bulging, his eyes rolling back in his head. "*CART BREAKER! WATER-THIEF! CHI HIIIICCCCCCCCEEEEEENNNNNN...CHI HIIIICCC-CCCCEEEEEEENNNNNN... CHI HI!IICCCCCCCCEEEEEEENNNNNN!*"

And as Ravjah collapsed back into his son's arms, spent of all cosmic energy, I realized that he wasn't talking about the water cart... and never had been.

As his father shrunk in his arms like a plum in the sunshine, Purevdorj carefully took up the old man's weight and prepared to head back to Ravjah's ger. But before he did, Purevdorj turned around to give me a questioning glance.

"I didn't mean to," I said quietly. "But maybe I did break it after all."

And hanging my head in silence, I went back inside.

***

The old man died later that night.

The next day, I invited myself over to Tsetseg's ger for a cup of tea. At first, my counterpart didn't want to talk about Ravjah's death - or even death in general - but after a little pestering, I talked her into explaining the next steps of the Mongol burial process.

"Mongols do not like to talk about death and... how do you say... ghosts?" Tsetseg told me, shaking her head. "These are not things you need to know."

"These are *exactly* the things I need to know," I replied. "Please."

Although there is no Mongol equivalent to the American "please", my counterpart had learned that the word held a special meaning. So making a clicking noise that let me know I was being stupid, Tsetseg acquiesced and told me what would happen to Ravjah:

First the lama would undress the corpse and pour milk over Ravjah's body, watching for any distinct patterns in the spilt milk. That way, if a baby were ever born with the exact same pattern, the family would know the child was Ravjah's reincarnation. Prayers would be said, and the family would say their goodbyes. Later, the lama would collect the body and lead the male family members out a secret burial spot in the khuudo, which he had personally selected days before as Ravjah's final resting place. There the body would be interred, and a small headstone would be erected.

And that was that, Tsetseg said. But then she thought for a moment, and began to speak again.

However, in the old days, there were no gravestones... or even graves. A corpse was simply taken out to the steppe and left for the wild dogs and birds to eat, returning them to the great cycle of energy and providing a poor animal with a life-saving meal. But over the last hundred years, as the changing Mongolian culture began to shame them out of the practice, the villagers began to bury their dead in shallow plots and mark them with concrete or iron plaques. And over those years, a small graveyard was built... or accumulated, depending on how you see it.

When I tried to ask about the location of these graves, Tsetseg stopped me before I could finish my sentence.

"You cannot go there," she said emphatically. "It is only a place for dead people and their families."

"What's the big deal?" I asked. "In America, graveyards are open to the public. Sometimes they're even tourist spots."

Tsetseg shook her head. "This is not America, and not for tourists. I have already said too much. But this is the truth... do not look for bones that are not yours. Do not go to the graveyard. Do you UNDERSTAND?"

And all of the sudden, I realized that my counterpart was serious.

Although their population is listed as being predominantly "Buddhist", as a whole, most of the Mongolians I'd met so far were lukewarm on the dogma of formal religion. The Dansarans had a framed portrait of Buddha on the wall for instance, but I never saw a single one of them so much as glance at a sutra the whole summer we were in Delgerkhovd. In fact, the only times that I ever saw Mongolians practice traditional Buddhism were at birth and death... much like the average Christian only remembers their faith during Christmas and election years.

Instead, the true spiritual force that rules the Mongol people can best be described as a superstitious paganism that the western world has largely dismissed as "old wives" tales... the thousand secret religions of Mongolia. These superstitions guide the rural Mongolian's life as surely as a lighthouse guides a freighter through a foggy sea, and an egregious violation of any of them can turn a Peace Corps volunteer into a social pariah.

A hat can never be placed upside down, or bad luck will surely come to the owner. Light from a full moon cannot touch a pregnant woman's stomach, for risk of miscarriage. Exchanging money on a Tuesday means certain financial woes. Stepping on the ger threshold is serious bad juju, and was even punishable by death during the reign of Chingiis Khaan. Spilling milk is akin to breaking a dozen mirrors. Whistling inside of a home can attract bad spirits (and is simply impolite). Etcetera, etcetera, etcetera...

And a warning not to visit a Mongol graveyard is to be disobeyed at one's own peril.

For a while, Tsetseg and I sat there at her table, feeling anew the cultural void that still lay between us. And it was apparent to me then, that no matter how well I assimilated to Mongolia, or how many lepers I healed (if any), there would always be an invisible and insurmountable wall between us that I could never completely cross.

I took a sip of my tea, which had grown cold.

Tsetseg countered with a sip of hers.

"I promise not to visit the graveyard," I finally said.

"That is good," Tsetseg replied.

And we sat for a long while then, in silence.

***

As it turned out, the worst part about wintertime Mongolia wasn't the frigid cold, or the loneliness, or even the death and desperation.

It was the boredom.

For the first few months, living in a ger had been romantic... swashbuckling... badass. For a while, the few comforts and habits that I had brought from America kept the worst of the cabin fever at bay. For a while, my guitar, journal and books kept the winds from growing too loud. For a while, my class work and lesson plans kept the darkness from swallowing me whole.

For a while.

But as time and winter slogged onward, I began to lose my grip. The awful stillness of the Gobi nights hung around too long into the morning. I began to hold two-way conversations with myself. Eventually, as the winter grew worse and I was trapped indoors for 16 hours a day, the whole crazy situation birthed a strange paranoia in the back of my mind, a state existing somewhere between cabin fever and Aspberger's Syndrome.

And then one day, just as I'd reached the end of all human tolerance for solitaire, I found my salvation.

I was buying smokes at one of the tiny, village shops when I first saw it. It was lying on the bottom shelf, a tiny, square thing with a dented antenna, about the size of a toaster and with scratched, plastic paneling, the sort of thing that you'd find in the discount rack of a thrift shop, too antiquated to use and not broken enough to throw away.

"Is that a radio?" I asked the shopkeeper, amazed at what I was seeing.

"*Tiggie tiggie...* of course, it's a radio," he told me, speaking slowly in Mongolian so I could understand. "It's a very good radio. But I can't sell this thing... because there are no... there are no..."

And he mimed out radio waves with his hands.

"Signals," I said in English, unsure of the Mongol translation.

"*Sig-nals*," he repeated, "*Mandalzuud. Beesh. Beckwhey.*"

This was something that I had realized long ago. While many of the larger cities and aimag centers of Mongolia had a local radio station or two, it was the rare Gobi village that was within range of more than an occasional static fart. Mandalzuud was no exception; it wasn't able to pick up a single goddamn thing.

And we all knew this.

The logical conclusion was that buying a transistor radio in Mandalzuud was about as useful as buying socks for a jellyfish. But the winter madness had begun to take its toll, and I thought back to my ger, where the *same* goddamn books awaited me, the *same* goddamn guitar sat under my bed, the *same* goddamn mp3 player shuffled the *same* goddamn songs over and over and over and over...

And that's how I ended up spending a week's food money on a radio.

***

Of course, when I took the radio home and tried it out, I couldn't get a single sound out of the thing. But this didn't stop me from spending hours fumbling around with the dial and antenna, hoping in vain and monotony to get some signal... any signal... be it music or mumbling or madness.

Using a length of metal wire that I extracted from the spine of a notebook, I attempted to make an antenna extension, coiling the wire around the radio's own antenna like a vine around a tree trunk. Taking the radio and hitting the road, I tried to pick up signals at different locations, heights, surroundings and weather. I searched the bandwidth systematically at different times of day, waking myself up in the wee hours of the morning for a full week to check for stray signals. I kept a log book, carefully planning my airwave searches to avoid duplication of effort. But day after day, despite my fevered search, I continued to be greeted by nothing more than static.

I was nearly ready to add my radio to the village trash heap, when the solution was plopped right in my lap.

That day, I was sitting in the village school after classes had ended, having brought my radio to my classroom, determined to add another location (school, classroom #4) and time (Tuesday, 4:30 p.m.) to the log book. I had found nothing – as usual - and was about to pack up my things and go home, when I heard a timid voice call to me from the classroom doorway.

I turned to see Jargal, one of my fourth grade students, standing there holding in a laugh.

"Teacher," she said in Mongolian, pointing at the radio. "That will not work here."

I rolled my eyes and answered her in Mongol. "Yes, Jargal. Thanks. Why are you here?"

"I will go to the khuudo tomorrow, and will not come to class. Zuger-oo?"

"Zuger," I said, giving her the thumbs up.

Jargal nodded her thanks, and stealing one last giggling look at my radio, she turned to leave the classroom. "*Bagsha...* you are silly. There is only one place in Mandalzuud where you can hear the radio."

"What?" I blurted out, looking up from my desk. "Where?"

Jargal squinted, confused by my sudden interest.

"Did you say that there's a place where the radio works in Mandalzuud?" I repeated.

She nodded, not understanding why I was asking such a simple question.

"Well, where is it?" I asked, trying not to sound too fervent.

And as soon as Jargal told me where to find a radio signal, I knew that the answer had been right under my nose the entire time:

The Mandalzuud Cell Phone Ovoo.

***

Ovoos – huge heaps of stones that stand anywhere from a few feet to twice the height of a man - are one of the secret religions of Mongolia.

Built on the peaks of mountains and at important cross-roads, the massive rock piles are immensely useful as land-marks, especially in the spacious and indistinguishing parts of the steppe. In fact, in the back country, a large ovoo will often be the only readily identifiable signpost within kilometers. But ovoos are much more than Mongolian GPS. Like little, nomadic churches, they represent something shamanistic... something spiritual. Many ovoos are decorated by a *khadaad* scarves, which are mounted on broom handles and hung like flags upon the rock piles. Some ovoos are adorned with artis-tically stacked animal skulls, or other sacred-looking bits of rubble. Often, visiting Mongols will leave tiny offerings at the base of an ovoo - candy, money, vodka - in hopes that their journey will be blessed. But perhaps the most amazing tradition surrounding ovoos is this: any Mongol passing one of the sacred rock cairns must circle it three times, adding a stone to the pile each time. In this way, an ovoo is literally a product of hundreds of pairs of hands... a thousand-person poem that is constantly evolving... a solitary snowflake... a fingerprint of God.

Still, to the outside observer, ovoos are not much to behold. Their simplicity is their greatest camouflage. In fact - to the foreign eye - an ovoo is little more than a curious pile of rocks.

But then again, so is a church.

***

The Mandalzuud Cell Phone Ovoo was located at the top of a lonesome hill, a half-mile outside our village. None of the villagers knew who constructed it, but the thing was clearly built with magic in mind.

While most ovoos are built haphazardly at best, Mandalzuud Cell Phone Ovoo was meticulously stacked, about four feet high and twice as deep. A walking path of white stones ran up the hill to the rock pile, looping around in a circle and continuing back down the mountain on the other side. And most eerily of all, a geometrically stacked formation of horse skulls was laid in front of the ovoo rock pile... which pointed in a triangle at a spot near the hill's peak.

The first time Tsetseg took me out to the Cell Phone Ovoo, I was struck mute in amazement. The hill was low, no higher than a couple hundred feet, and as far as I knew there weren't any underground metal deposits around that could amplify a signal. I looked in the distance towards the faraway village of Mandalgobi, the closest possible place a radio tower could be. Mandalzuud lay at least fifty kilometers beyond any signal that their tiny radio station could put out, or any other radio station in the vicinity for that matter. There was no logical, scientific explanation... but somehow, there it was... magic... magic... magic.

Because here - standing in the exact right position - a person could pick up a single bar of cell phone reception.

***

It was for this reason that I set off for the Cell Phone Ovoo the next day, radio in hand.

Jargal had assured me that – just like cell phones – radios could also pick up stray signals on top of that holy hill. It should have been something that I figured out earlier. But then again, who the hell in their right mind would make that terrible trip in the middle of wintertime Mongolia just to sit out in the freezing gales and listen to the goddamn radio?

So as soon as school was over, I set off for the Cell Phone Ovoo to hunt for a signal. The journey was terrible. Garbed in my U.S. Post Office issued coat and two layers of clothes, I had also brought a wool blanket from my ger, which I wrapped around my head and body like a Bedouin herder. Yet after only ten minutes, my eyes were already watering, my nose was numb, and my fingers were beginning to stiffen like claws around the handle of my radio. When I reached the top of the hill, I walked over to the rock cairn and set my radio down directly in front of the skull pile.

Shivering inside my coat, I turned it on and scanned the AM bandwidth. Finding nothing, I turned to the FM stations. At first, I was greeted by the same, mocking white noise... nothing through the high eighties... nothing through the low nineties... nothing... nothing...

And around 95.3 fm, I heard it.

I had almost skipped over the station altogether, thinking that it was some trick of the wind. But for some instinctive reason my hand lingered on the dial, and after a moment and a little fine tuning, I realized what I was hearing...

Voices.

They were only tinny, far-off echoes, too distant to decipher for content or context - like poor-quality astronaut transmissions from the moon - but they were definitely voices, and that was enough to startle me into action. Quickly, I took my wire-coil antenna from out of my pocket and attached it to the radio. I grasped the end of the antenna with my hand, using my own body as a conductor.

Together, the radio and I joined souls.

And as we did, the voices became clear, as if there were three other people sitting there on that hilltop with me. Cities connected. Continents bridged. The world became as one. And all of the sudden, I was no longer alone.

That's when I realized that I was listening to a Chinese radio talk show.

To this day, I had no idea what those men were discussing... sports, the weather, atom bombs... it could have been anything. But somehow, it didn't matter. I crouched on that frigid hilltop for nearly an hour, huddled up in my blanket with my radio at my feet, listening to those Chinese men talk Chinese at each other while I grinned like an idiot. That one broadcast, wherever it had come from, had stirred up a thousand separate memories in my mind... Casey Kasem and my first cigarette, the first time I'd heard Dylan play "Tangled Up in Blue", sitting in a meadow on my grandparent's farm in Sussex County with a double-A battery radio listening to Jethro Tull on local FM... good memories... good living.

All this time, I had just accepted that there was no radio to listen to in Mandalzuud. It was like accepting that there was no plumbing, or running water, or cable TV or pizza delivery. But hearing that Gobi talk show had put the radio back into the realm of the possible, and I found myself returning to the same question, over and over again...

What would it be like if Mandalzuud had radio?

I imagined hordes of Mongols gathered around a boombox at the delguur, grooving to some Creedence Clearwater Revival... an emergency broadcast weather system that could save lives and livestock... a "Live From Mandalzuud" concert series... a political talk forum... village-wide English lessons... free exchange of information... true democracy... the fourth estate... and music, sweet music, all the hours of the day.

But most of all, I thought of salvation.

And that's how I decided to build a radio station.

$$\sim 12 \sim$$

How to Build a Pirate Radio Station in Mongolia

With three simple components - a transmitter, an antenna and a microphone – even the most technically impaired revolutionary can construct their very own pirate radio station.

The concept is simple:

You speak into the microphone. The sound waves from your voice are run through the transmitter, which turns them into electromagnetic ripples. These ripples are then amplified and sent scattering through the stratosphere via your antenna. The invisible messages pulse through the air - like wrinkles from a stone cast into a pond - until a faraway radio recognizes them and pulls them in.

And then - miraculously - your goddamn voice reappears out of nowhere, a hundred miles away.

It's a concept so simple, people have been doing it for nearly a half-century in every situation imaginable... from the ham radio operator in his suburban bedroom, to the South American revolutionary in the middle of a jungle. In the United States, an enterprising individual can slap together a low powered radio station in a week, maybe less, presuming he or she is willing to go pirate.

In Mongolia, I figured that it would take me about six months.

Six months to build a radio station, I thought. *Six months to find The Answer.*

Six months to freedom.

Ha.

***

Like heroin rehab, the first step towards actualizing my radio station was admitting my own nakedness. This meant coming to grips with my most serious limitation... after all my time in Mandalzuud and all my efforts to blend in, I was still technically an "outsider."

It was clear that I needed local help to pull my plan off... and that meant involving my Corps counterpart, Tsetseg. Without her translating assistance and personal connections, the whole concept of a Mandalzuud radio station was all only the silly whim of an American, no more substantial than a fairy tale or the millions of "good intentions" that line the waiting room walls of Purgatory. So over Sunday tea, armed with dozens of blueprints, schematics, diagrams, flow charts, budget estimates and goal statements (all the products of cabin fever in wintertime Mongolia), I laid out the entire vision to my counterpart.

To her credit, Tsetseg took the whole crazy notion in stride.

"How much will this cost?" was all she asked.

"In the States, it would cost about five or six thousand bucks to do a job like this from scratch, plus broadcasting license fees, of course." I told my counterpart. "I'm willing to bet that in Mongolia, we can do it for half of that... presuming that we're willing to go pirate."

"Pirate?"

"Meaning we don't worry about getting a license," I explained.

"Ah – yes – well, that is still *many* tugrugs," Tsetseg asked me. "We can get this money?"

"Sure," I said. "The Peace Corps has a network of grants for this type of thing. There's all sorts of money laying around, just waiting for people like us to grab it. How hard could it be to raise a few thousand dollars, anyway?"

My counterpart laughed. "Yes, I forgot. You are American."

"What do you mean by that?" I asked, pretending to be offended.

Tsetseg patted my hand and smiled. "*Oochlaraay.* This is bad humor, I think."

"But what do you think of the *idea*?" I asked. "That's the important thing. Do you think this would be good for Mandalzuud? Do we need radio? Or will we be better off building an English library or something?"

Tsetseg nodded in affirmation. I waited for her to elaborate, but she volunteered nothing.

"Are you sure?" I re-queried.

She nodded again. "You are the Peace Corps volunteer, Eric. We trust."

As I looked into my counterpart's eager, shining face, I saw that she really *did* trust me. And with this simple realization, all my original reasons for coming to Mongolia came zooming back like little boomerangs.

"Thanks," I told my counterpart, oversimplifying yet again. "That really means a lot."

Tsetseg smiled. "*Zuger.* But there is one thing I cannot help you with..."

She told me that many of the more common items we would need - a CD player, a small 4-channel mixing board, some CDs, furniture for the station - would be easy to get, as long as we made a trip to the capitol city. The problem was going to be finding a radio transmitter. For that matter, I didn't know where the hell we were going to get a quality radio antenna either, and getting hold of those two items out in the middle of the Gobi wasn't going to be as simple as going down to the local Radio Shack.

My counterpart and I looked at each other in silence for a moment.

"Maybe one of the radio stations in Ulaanbaatar can tell us where they got *their* equipment," I said, trying to sound confident.

Tsetseg nodded. "We will call them at the post office. Then we will see."

***

In the end, it took a little arm twisting to get the info we needed.

The first three radio stations that we called swore that they "didn't remember" where they got their equipment. It was only after I lost my temper and started yelling about being under the authority of "the goddamn United States Peace Corps", that one station manager finally took pity on me. According to him, their station had bought their transmitter and antenna from an expatriate Russian tinkerer named Alexei, who ran a small electronics store in Ulaanbaatar. The Russian spoke three languages - one of them English – which I took as a sign that I was on the right track.

"Just don't tell him that you're American," the station manager warned me.

"Huh?" I asked. "Why?"

"Just don't," was all he said.

The next day I went down to the post office and called the number the manager had given us. After a few rings, a gruff and suspicious voice answered.

"*Chto vy khotityay?*" it demanded in Russian, switching abruptly to Mongolian. "*Khen be?*"

"I am looking for Alexei," I said, slowly. "I want to buy a radio transmitter."

The voice paused in surprise, temporarily stunned by the brute power of English.

"I am Alexei," he slowly admitted in a thick accent after a moment. "Please excuse... I have not speak English for long time. Who are you?"

"My name is Eric. Our friend, Munkhbat from 100.7 FM, told me to call."

I waited a moment for Alexei to recognize the name, but he only continued breathing into the receiver, saying nothing.

"I want to build a radio station," I said, "And Munkhbat told me that you sell FM radio transmitters and antennas. I would like to buy one of each."

For a moment, Alexei was silent, and I briefly wondered if he had understood me at all. But after a moment he began to hum to himself and I could tell that he was simply thinking, so I waited patiently until he stopped.

"Hmmmm... Munkhbat, ehhhh?" the Russian said at last. "You want to buy transmitter and antenna? True. I build. Sometimes expensive. But very good."

I paused, trying to keep my voice casual. "So how much money would this cost?"

"How big?"

"A hundred watts. Maybe a hundred and fifty."

"Antenna, too?"

I told him yes.

Alexei sucked in his breath and clicked his tongue against his teeth; I waited silently.

"For transmitter and antenna, I need three million tugrugs," he finally told me, his voice lead-solid.

I did the tugrug to dollar conversion in my head... *about twenty-three hundred bucks.* Absolutely reasonable, assuming it was quality equipment.

"How long would it take you to build?" I asked.

Alexei snorted. "I have many transmitters like this now. You get tomorrow, if you like."

"Well, I don't have the money right *now*," I explained, "I just wanted to know how much it would be."

As soon as he heard I had no money, Alexei sucked in his breath.

"You... have... no... money?" the Russian asked, trying to confirm what he had just heard. I could tell that he was trying not to yell.

"Well, I *will*..." I said, scrambling to explain our situation. "You see, I'll have the funds as soon as the grants are approved, but the Peace Corps won't let us apply for grants until we go to a special training seminar in February, so I need to wait until then to apply for a grant, which will take another month or two before we get approved, but we should have funding in about..."

Mercifully, Alexei stopped me before I could rattle off another sentence.

"You call again please, American friend, when you have money," he said, trying to end the conversation. "*Dosvadanya.*"

"Wait a second!" I exclaimed, more to myself than to Alexei. "How did you know that I'm American?"

The Russian clicked his tongue in irritation. "What other people shop with no money?"

And he hung up the phone.

***

The last piece to our radio station was finding a location.

Our list of demands was short. We needed a place with electricity and heat, somewhere high up and dry. We needed a place that was in the center of town, accessible to everyone in the village and politically neutral. We needed a place that would inspire community... sharing... communication... truth.

But more importantly, we needed a place that was free.

When I first brought up the issue to Tsetseg, my counterpart had nodded to me and told me that she might know a place.

"We can use the Ghost Room," she told me.

"The what?" I asked.

Tsetseg clicked her tongue. "The post office has a... how do you say... attic? When the building was first made, they tried to build an extra room above to use as an office. But in the middle of work, they ran out of money. Mongolian projects *always* run out of money. Now the room sits empty, with no paint, no electricity, no chairs or tables. The post office workers call it the 'Ghost Room'. But I think that if we ask, they will let us use it."

"All we must do," she concluded, "is ask."

"Hot damn!" I exclaimed, excitedly slapping Tsetseg on the shoulder. "Hot damn! Good work, counterpart!"

She smiled gratefully, sharing my sudden enthusiasm. "And of course, we must ask Boldbaatar if we can use it. I can do this, myself, if you like."

I stopped my celebration in its tracks. "Who? Did you say Boldbaatar?"

Boldbaatar, the village governor, was the resident Boss Hogg of Mandalzuud. A large and dynamic man who loved to slam his fist on nearby tables as he spoke, he was undeniably charismatic... in a Fourth Reich sort of way. The man was unapologetic and forceful, a Mongolian version of Marlon Brando. (Such ciphers of human bullishness are adored in Mongolia.) But underneath the bravado and posturing, Boldbaatar had a cunning intelligence that I hadn't seen for a long time... not since America.... and I didn't like it in the slightest. It was the predatory acumen of a corporate raider, a Wall Street day trader, a self-help motivational speaker. It was eye intelligence, a reptile wisdom that was constantly weighing consequence against morality.

And I wanted nothing to do with the man.

Tsetseg nodded, still excited from my previous outburst. "*Tiggie*... yes, of course. The village government pays for the post office to stay open. So the village governor must approve."

I closed my eyes, and pinched the bridge of my nose with my forefingers. "Boldbaatar," I muttered, shaking my head dejectedly. "Can't we just ask the postal workers if it's OK?"

Tsetseg shook her head. "No... this must be done. The postal workers are not in charge, they are only workers. The village government... how do you say... *owns* the post office. We must ask Boldbaatar."

"Ah," I said.

My counterpart scrutinized me with sudden concern. "Why? Our governor is a nice man. He will help us. Is there a problem?"

"No problem at all," I said, hoping that she wouldn't be able to read my body language well enough to know that I was lying.

***

Much to my surprise, the bastard loved the idea.

As soon as we told Boldbaatar about the project, I could see that he was sold before we even got our foot in the door. As I pitched our idea and Tsetseg translated, the village governor chuckled to himself giddily. I showed him the blueprints, schematics, diagrams, flow charts, budget estimates and goal statements. I told him about the free press, and responsible media, and community radio. I promised that I would find funding for the project.

And all the while, I watched for his response.

"Yes, yes," he repeated over and over, rubbing his hands together, working the living hell out of the only words of English that he knew. "Radio... radio."

When I had finished my pitch, Boldbaatar leaned over and spoke to Tsetseg in soft and rapid Mongolian. I couldn't quite make out what he was saying, but I overheard something about "questions" and "leadership." As the governor spoke, Tsetseg's face brightened into a banana split smile. After a minute or so, Boldbaatar slowed down, concluded his speech, and sat back in his chair. He sat there, hands folded on the desktop, staring back at me like a bank officer interviewing a bankrupt loan candidate.

And grinning, he held up two fingers.

"What?" I asked, looking at the dopey smirks on the two Mongolian's faces.

"Boldbaatar thinks that a radio station will be *great* for Mandalzuud," Tsetseg said excitedly. "The village government will let us use the Ghost Room... yes... and will even pay for electricity and heat."

"Really?" I asked, looking incredulously at both of them.

They nodded in unison.

"What's the catch?" I asked.

Tsetseg smiled at my use of American idiom. "*Nothing* is the catch. Our governor believes that a radio station would be very useful to the village. It is something that he has wanted for a long time, but has not had the time or money to do. Boldbaatar only wants to ask you two questions, and then he will give us his approval."

"Two questions?" I asked, looking at the governor, numb in disbelief that it was going to be this easy. "Shoot."

Tsetseg clicked her tongue. "The Peace Corps will pay for all equipment, is this true?"

"Well, it's a little more complicated than that, and it won't be the Peace Corps that actually gives us the money... but yes," I said, nodding. "We'll have to find a 'grant'... money that someone is willing to give us... but the Peace Corps has all sorts of connections and donors that they can funnel our way. In fact, there's a special Peace Corps workshop coming up in a little while, and once it's over, I'll be able to start applying for some of these grants. It'll take a few months, but I personally promise that the government will not have to pay a cent... beyond electricity and heat, that is... and that's totally up to him. We just need the room. What's the second question?"

Tsetseg hesitated for the slightest of seconds. "The governor wants to know who will be the radio station *darga*..."

"*Darga?*" I asked, confused.

"Darga means the person in charge. The boss."

"Well..." I said, scratching my head, "Like I told you guys in my proposal, I think that we should have a democratically elected station manager. We can have a vote among the station volunteers, and whoever gets the most votes wins... good, old fashioned majority-takes-all politics. But why does it matter, if he doesn't mind my asking?"

Tsetseg translated my question to Boldbaatar, who responded without hesitation.

"Boldbaatar said that Mongolians like to have someone in charge. It is part of our heritage. It is the way things work in Mongolia. We must have a darga," my counterpart said.

I paused, looking at the governor from across his desk. For a second, I felt a twinge of suspicion, like a dog that suddenly gets the idea that he's about to be kicked. But as quick as it came, the feeling passed, and I remembered that this was not just a radio station we were talking about... it was redemption.

"If he promises to help us build this radio station," I finally said, looking back at Tsetseg, "We can appoint a king, for all I care."

As soon as it was translated, this answer seemed to satisfy the governor, and he rose from his seat and reached out to conclude our conversation with a handshake.

"*Rah-dio*," he told me, as his meaty paw engulfed my hand.

"Radio," I agreed.

And like that, our fates were linked.

~ 13 ~

The Dead Dog Reunion

The great Mongol city of Ulaanbaatar - "U.B." as the tourists call it - is a hobbling, pimply teenager.

With one foot firmly planted in the modern age, and one foot dragging lamely behind in the preindustrial past, U.B. is a strange dichotomy. Home to a whopping forty percent of the nation's population, it is a city that recently built its first privately-owned shopping mall, yet half of its citizens still live in slums without electricity or plumbing.

And both sides are still fighting it out, to see who gets to ruin Mongolia first.

The city is, without a doubt, the friendliest place for an expatriate in the entire nation... if you have the money. It is a place where you can see a dentist or order a deep-dish pizza. It is a place where the banks have video cameras. It is a place where you can take a hot shower and have a freshly brewed cup of coffee. It is a place of curiosity... contortionist strippers and Tuvaan throat-singers, erotic "fashion" shows in dingy nightclubs, Buddhist temples and state-sponsored Mongolian Opera. Here, you can buy a big screen TV, an ipod battery charger or a plane ticket home. Here, the restaurants serve steak.

But the underbelly of U.B. is a different story.

Past the tourist-friendly State Department Store and Sukhbaatar Square, the streets are filled with unemployable refugees of the modern world - all with no money in their pockets - who gather in vast slums in the "Ger Districts" of the city. In these slums, the citizens of U.B. turn the skies black with coal and garbage fires, and the sun is spoken of in the past tense. Here, a volunteer can put their Corps-taught knowledge of pickpockets to good use. Here, a thousand, homeless beggar children live in the sewer system below the city, and dressed in tattered rags and sniffling with cancer, periodically emerge from the underground like trained rats to sadly sing on street corners for money until the thuggish City Police chase them away.

Here, the wealth has clearly not trickled down.

This strange dichotomy of rich and poor... modern and antique... creates a social tapestry that is unlike any other in the world. Ah, U.B. She is a city of phlegm coughs and slamming doors and rusting iron. She is a city of disco bars and not-so-quiet urban desperation. She is a city where every surface is peeling and every sidewalk is cracked. She is a city that runs on pennies a day. She is a city where "industrialization" has turned whole generations of the greatest nomadic culture in human history into taxi drivers, shoe shiners, kiosk dwellers and day laborers.

Yet in the end, she is a city that McDonalds still refuses to open a franchise in.

***

In late February, the Corps brought our entire volunteer class back to U.B. for the mandatory Project Design and Management seminar (PDM), a week-long course designed to teach us the finer points of begging the U.S. government for grant money. And so the M-17 Peace Corps class reunited... sweeping in from the four corners of the nation... crawling out from under our rocks... bedraggled and dusty... sick and hollow in a thousand different ways... all heading for the same, glorious-sounding city of Ulaanbaatar.

That year, the Corps hosted the seminar at a posh tourist resort called Nukht, located on the still-pristine Eastern foothills of the city. The resort stood in jutting contrast to the honking, brawling neighborhoods of the city. At Nukht, we were treated to a catered dining hall, a lounge with a big screen TV, a downstairs dance club, daily maid service and mini-bars in each room... expatriate living at its finest. The Corps termed this "mental therapy", and we all breathed a sigh of relief when we found out that our rooms had adjustable thermostats and private showers. Even the most grizzled among us needed a respite, not because our new life-styles were that difficult on a basic human level, but because we had all been so ill-prepared for them.

How many Americans, after all, will ever need to wash laundry by hand? Or start a fire with dung chips? Or learn how to piss in a sandstorm?

But I sat around Nukht that week, sipping on cups of hotel coffee and sleeping on clean sheets, it gradually dawned on me that the money the Corps had spent on this week-long orgy could have completely paid for a dozen of our projects at site. *We could have funded a domestic abuse center with this money*, I thought, as I lounged around Nukht like a sultan with the other volunteers. *We could have founded an independent newspaper, or built a public computer lab. But here we are, pocket change humanists, scrounging around for a few thousand bucks to fund our awful little attempts at saving the world, spending all of our money trying to learn how to get a little of it back.*

Perhaps it was all designed to be this way. I remembered reading a story about the end of World War II, when the Russian army had begun to run out of ammunition, leaving many of its soldiers with guns but no bullets. The Russian commanders made these men charge with guns raised anyway, with the orders that they yell out "BANG" as they approached, in order to distract the Germans' attention from any soldier who still had bullets.

BANG BANG, MOTHERFUCKER, I whispered to myself, as I looked around at the catered meals, the conference rooms, the two-ply toilet tissue.

BANG BANG.

***

In reality, the Peace Corps' *true* interest in bringing us back to U.B. was not to teach us how to manage grants. There is very little damage an American can do with $4,000, after all. No... the Corps' real reason for hosting the Projects Design and Management seminar is simple.

They want to check their first-year volunteers for insanity.

And in the end, I couldn't say that I blamed them. Our time on-site had changed us all. For example, most of us had given up on the American standard of hygiene long ago. Half of the men now sported what was dubbed the "Jesus Beard", an unkempt (but holy-looking) patchwork of facial stubble. Half of the women hid their hairy legs under sweat pants and jeans, bursting at the seams for the opportunity to shave, but the others declared loudly and proudly that they just didn't give a damn anymore. I could count the number of volunteers that still bathed daily on one hand. Most of the men in our group had lost ten pounds. Most of the women had gained the same. Our clothing had rips and cigarette burns, our boots were beginning to lose their treads, and almost all our fingernails were dirty and chipped. The attractive people had gotten uglier; the ugly people had grown more beautiful.

And yet, these physical changes were only the tip of the iceberg.

We had seen *things*, some beautiful and some terrible, but all pan-seared into our hearts with extreme prejudice and love, and all impossible to ignore. Our environments had begun to stain our countenances... the altitude and wood-chopping duties of the Altai Mountains, the rock star life of an American in Ulaanbaatar, the sun and sands of the Gobi, the tranquility of the Khovsgul lakes in the north. We wore our homes on our faces: impossible-to-blend sunglass tans, noses that no longer twitched at the smell of dung, eyebrows worn thin from stress and hunger, pairs of bleary eyes that no longer blinked when they stared at the sun.

We had all been molested... most of us by demons, but a few of us by angels as well.

And it showed.

***

When I met the remaining members of the Delgerkhovd Seven, they were all transformed souls.

Eddie - the aspiring National Geographic photographer from Vermont - was now more camera than man. At Nukht, he showed me some pictures that he'd taken of the village governor's handmade, deerskin ger. The tent's interior was lined with dozens of pelts... beautiful, furry things with muted spots like a cheetah, but with a delicate, silvery outline of white fur around the edges.

It took me a moment before I realized what species they were.

"Jesus shit, man," I said, crooking an eyebrow. "Are those snow leopards?"

Eddie nodded.

"The endangered species? About a hundred of the fuckers left in the wild?"

Eddie nodded. A long while passed.

"They must have been some goddamn things to look at when they were alive," I finally said, handing Eddie's pictures back.

"They're *still* some goddamn things to look at," he said, his left eye twitching involuntarily from camera withdrawal. "Everything is *always* beautiful, when you look at it through a camera lens."

***

Ray, the professor's son, had been given the task of running an English prep program at a school in Ulaanbaatar. His initial assignment was to build a complete English library, stocked with all the teaching materials he could find. That's when Ray first noticed the phenomena that he later dubbed, "Book Museum Syndrome."

"When I first built that library, everyone at the school all acted like I had just completed an ark before the flood arrived," Ray told me at Nukht, his eyes ripe with the memory.

"They had a little ceremony to commemorate the opening... the students put on this play for me... the principal's wife sewed me a new del. You would have thought that I'd built a golden statue of Chingiis Khan. And I know it's stupid, but the whole thing really made me feel good about myself, like I had finally made some sort of difference, you know? It wasn't until a few weeks later that I noticed something funny... nobody had been reading any of the books. They'd just been sitting on the shelves the whole time, displayed in their bookcases like trophies. When I went to the librarian, I asked why nobody was using the English library. 'Oh, we don't take those books out of the cases,' she said. 'Why not?' I asked. And do you know what she said to me?"

"THESE BOOKS ARE TOO NICE TO READ."

Ray laughed. "Man, my dad went to Ghana during the JFK days of the Peace Corps – the badass days – and he helped to build a bridge. A goddamn bridge! And what did I accomplish? I built a Book Museum. I don't think I ever really understood the meaning of that until now."

And right up to his resignation from the Corps, that was all Ray would say about that.

***

Abbie, on the other hand, was on her way to becoming a little Buddha.

The skater chick from Washington had ended up in the far eastern province of Khentii, and had been getting involved with the restoration of a local Buddhist temple near her village. To thank Abbie for her efforts, a monk at the temple offered to teach her Vipassana meditation on the weekends. His lessons had proved rewarding. Abbie returned to U.B. with an amazing aura of slow awareness... light years removed from the slightly skittish girl in the Against All Authority tour jacket that we knew before she headed out to site. The proof was in her voice... deeper yet more feminine... slowed from a Screeching Weasel soprano to an "Om" chant alto.

Curious, I cornered her one night at Nukht and asked her what her secret was.

She shrugged. "It's not going to be an answer that you want."

"Try me," I said.

"When I first arrived in my village, I asked Adnaa, the monk who teaches me meditation, why there was so much suffering in the world. He told me that Mongolians believe there are three kinds of darkness... Dark is the night without the moon... Dark is the mind of the scattered... Dark is the sheep-yard without sheep. At first, I had no clue what he was talking about. But after half a year at site, I think that I've finally figured it out."

"What?" I asked.

"Suffering," Abbie asserted, "is overrated."

"That's it?" I queried, squinting in confusion.

"That's it," the little Buddha replied, flashing me a smile.

***

Vinko the Adventurer had ended up in the Dundgobi, only a few hundred kilometers from me. As such, he was my de facto, next-door, desert neighbor, although in the far places of Mongolia, a hundred kilometers might as well be a thousand.

When I saw Vinko in U.B., his hands were calloused, his face lean, his eyes endlessly fixated on some faraway mirage that nobody else but me could see. He spoke slowly, and walked with a slightly plodding slide because he was used to walking in sand, and when he was outside, he would often stop dead in his tracks to enjoy a sudden breeze. Since returning to Ulaanbaatar he had nearly been run down by a car a dozens of times.

It was clear that the Gobi had fucked up the Croatian's head a little bit... just like it had done to me.

But I would learn more about that, later.

***

The only one missing from the reunion was Bridget. The redhead had been kicked out of the Peace Corps - a month before PDM - for causing a public spectacle.

It all began when Bridget and an M-16 volunteer from the previous year's Corps class had gone out drinking at a disco club in U.B. Together, the two pretty, drunken white girls were the center of attention, and when a young Mongolian man with a camera began to take their pictures, they just grinned, gave their sexiest poses and held up their beer bottles.

A week later their photo appeared in a local newspaper. The caption read, "U.S. Peace Corps Volunteers Enjoy Cass Beer!" Twelve days later, Bridget and her friend were on a plane back to the United States, dismissed from the Peace Corps for "misrepresenting Peace Corps values and endangering the Peace Corps' mission."

But all in all, Bridget had a vacation that she wouldn't forget, and that was her main reason for coming to Mongolia in the first place. And in a way, I admired her for it.

If you have to go out... go out in a blaze of glory.

After all, it was *all* of our inner characters which had begun to emerge at site, forced from their shells like oysters pried apart by the blunt knife of Fate. We had *all* begun our transformations into the ideals we loved – or hated – the most. For many of us, hanging onto the past seemed almost masochistic, like we were flagellates whipping ourselves for the crimes of the world.

And a serious crackup for someone seemed to be inevitable at some point down the line.

***

In the end, it took four days worth of training sessions for the Corps to cover the project funding process.

The situation was not as encouraging as I had hoped.

The main problem was that most of the traditional sources of Peace Corps project funding - such as the U.S. "Wheat" grants - were drying up after the millennial humanitarianism boom of 2000. It turned out that the First World was forgetting the crazy promises that it had made back in 1999, when we all thought the world was going to end. Americans were no longer interested in spending money on things like "foreign aid" and "good will." And barely a decade later, now that the largest volunteer class in Peace Corps Mongolia history had arrived, all that was left of the millennium promise money was a motley assortment of rinky-dink government grants and private party solicitation schemes.

BANG BANG.

Many of the other volunteers would end up bypassing the whole goddamn charade altogether, simply turning to their friends and family in America for money to fund their projects. But as much as I wanted to, it somehow seemed like cheating. So in the end, I decided that the best chance for my Mandalzuud radio station seemed to lie with the United States Agency for International Development's "small project assistance grant."

The grants maxed out at about four grand, more than enough to build our station if I kept things cheap. Plus, according to several Peace Corps staff members, USAID was in a hurry to redistribute their latest cycle of funding before their budget was renewed. The entire process supposedly took about two months, leaving me on track to start purchasing equipment in May... presuming that Tsetseg and I sent out our grant application as soon as I returned to Mandalzuud.

Presuming also, I thought, *that they approve the goddamn thing in the first place.*

As I learned more about what USAID considered a typical project, I couldn't help but get a little worried. Over and over, I saw the same projects make the "best practice" lists: English libraries, computer labs, small business workshops... real Kissinger-and-Kinkade type shit... the kind of humanitarian projects that can be talked about on Voice of America radio and understood via logic model charts.

And here I was, about to ask for a few thousand bucks to build a pirate radio station.

But when the last PDM session was officially over, and we had finally been cleared to send out grant applications, I realized that things weren't that bad after all. After all this time at site, most of the other volunteers still had no idea what kind of projects they wanted to do, and if I hurried, I would almost certainly be the first to apply for a grant.

And more times than not, the funding formula was first come, first serve... kind of like the checkout line at Wal-Mart.

***

After our final night at Nukht, most of the other volunteers lingered around U.B. for another few days, getting drunk, eating pizza, shopping, going to the movies and occasionally meeting up to fornicate. Not even the cold of wintertime Ulaanbaatar was enough to deter them from their debauchery. For many, it was the last time they would be in U.B. for months - or even a year - and most of them wanted to drag out their time in the city for as long as possible.

Me on the other hand... I couldn't wait to get the fuck out of that terrible city.

During my time in the Gobi, I had begun to notice sensations that I had never experienced before... the sound of sand particles grinding against each other in the wind... the electrical charge of water on my skin... the laughter of snowfall against the roof of my ger. But ever since I had arrived in U.B., it was getting harder and harder to notice these things. I felt imbalanced, like I had gone swimming and got water clogged in my ears. I could already feel myself getting soft, gradually losing the edge that had taken me so long to earn in the Gobi. My mind was starting to react to the overkill of stimuli - the flashing lights and gaudy billboards and honking cars and shouting urbanites - and block out my environment rather than absorb it. After only a week in U.B., my senses were dulling. Things were starting to get complicated again.

And I knew that I had to flee as soon as possible before the city wrecked me.

Vinko the Adventurer - my closest Gobi neighbor - apparently felt the same way. Since he was headed in the same direction, we decided that it would make sense to take the trip together. We met at the bus depot the next day, blinking and disoriented in the voodoo February morning, shivering and with our breath fogging the air.

When I arrived at the depot, Vinko was standing over by a huge, unorganized crowd of passengers, waiting for the lone, Dundgobi-bound bus to open its door. The bus was ancient... Dis on wheels... little more than a sarcophagus held together by scotch tape and refrigerator magnets. Its hull was a color that might once have resembled a shade of blue but was now a hue very similar to Smurf vomit, and it was riddled with battle scars from major collisions and road shrapnel. It was an ugly thing with an ugly history, but so were most things headed for the Gobi.

There were clearly too many passengers to fit comfortably on the bus, which made for a mean and pushy crowd. Still, it was almost impossible to miss the tall Croatian; his head stood up above the melee like a redwood in a grove of sunflowers.

I waded through the morass of bodies and tapped him on the shoulder.

"That bus is a beauty, huh, dude?" I hollered at the back of his head.

Vinko startled for a second and his shoulder twitched, but he relaxed when he turned around and saw who had tapped him.

"Sorry man," he responded, relaxing and accepting my handshake, steam husking from his nostrils like an incensed yak. "I thought that you were a pickpocket. I was about to turn around and bitch slap you."

"No harm, no foul," I said curtly, as a sudden, cruel blast of February wind stopped our conversation short.

We waited in the cold for another fifteen minutes before the driver and his assistant - both stinking of vodka – decided that they had enough passengers and climbed aboard the bus. As the driver lit a cigarette and started up the engine, his assistant let the surging crowd onto the bus, collecting their fares as they pushed past like frenzied dinosaurs. I waited patiently with Vinko at the back of the group, watching my fellow passengers push and claw at each other to get on the bus, priding myself on my civility and dignity.

Naturally, when we finally got on the bus, there was no place left to sit.

So much for dignity, I thought.

When the driver's assistant came to Vinko and me, he stopped for a moment, giving us the hairy eyeball.

"*Khanaas irsen ve?*" the man said, his hairy lip trembling with make-believe authority, demanding to know where we were coming from.

"*Americaas,*" I answered, handing the man my fare. "*Enkh Tavnee Corpus.*"

"The Moon," Vinko said in English, returning the man's gaze with irritation, beating his hands against his arms for warmth. "I come from the Moon, you cheap bastard... what does it matter? Here's my goddamn money."

And he pressed his bills into the man's palm, and pushed his way onto the bus like all the others.

"I know that sounded intolerant, but this shit never ends!" Vinko complained, as the driver's assistant moved on to pester the other passengers. "I'm a six-foot-six, Croatian-American living in Mongolia... I've got to give my life story every time I want to buy a bar of soap. And now look... there's no place to goddamn sit!"

He was right; I counted at least forty passengers crammed into a space designed for twenty-five. They were every-where... two rows deep on the seats, perched on the steps by the door, and heaped onto each others' laps like bags of meat. The aisle was chock full of luggage... battered suitcases and duffel bags, burlap sacks of potatoes, hundred-pound hunks of semi-frozen beef that would thaw en route, large cardboard boxes of cheap consumer goods, ten gallon jugs of *aairag*.

A mouse didn't have room to shit in there.

We got on the bus and headed for the only open seat that wasn't on top of someone's lap or luggage... the bench in the back row without springs in the cushion... the seat that would rock with every dip of the road and roll with every yank of the steering wheel... the seat that even the Mongols hated... the Puke Seat.

"I hate this," I muttered, cramming my luggage underneath the seat.

"At least we *have* a seat to vomit in," Vinko said, smashing his luggage next to mine.

Eventually the bus was "full" and the passengers were all paid up, and the bus took off with a tremendous clatter, giving off a series of strained grunts, like a fat man pushing a bicycle up a steep hill. By bracing my head against the window and wedging myself as far into the corner as I could go, I managed to find a position that almost didn't make me feel like throwing up, and settled back to wait the journey out.

Zuger, zuger.

***

In five hours, our U.B.-bound bus arrived at Gwanztown, a strange, little settlement which subsisted solely on the bus traffic coming and going from Ulaanbaatar... the Gobi version of the Interstate rest stop.

Gwanztown wasn't much to look at. Its main offerings were a smattering of *gwanzes*... little, unlicensed mom and pop restaurants where a traveler could pick up a quick bite to eat. Next to the gwanzes were three or four *delguur* stores, which stocked little more than vodka, cigarettes, cookies and Cokes. Finally, there was an ancient, hand-cranked petrol pump that was operated by one of the delguurs... the only gas within six hundred kilometers.

I wasn't sure how many permanent residents there were in that place - if any - but it was obvious that Gwanztown was not a healthy place to linger. The village's inhabitants - a handful of nomad families and seedy-looking entrepreneurs - shuffled about with dull, coal-colored eyes. Their backs were stooped, their *dels* dirty, their hands yellow around the fingernails. Here and there, scrawny gwanz dogs wandered through town, their ribs jutting from their sides, fighting to the death over the pools of vomit that motion sick bus passengers left behind. The air was foul with idling bus exhaust, there was coughing everywhere, and every outhouse was overflowing. But most of all, there was a strange and slightly sad sense of flimsiness to the village, as if the whole place secretly wanted to uproot itself and move somewhere better... if only there was someplace better to go.

When our bus finally rattled to a stop, Vinko and I wandered off in a daze, receiving a stiff warning from the driver's assistant that the bus would be leaving in half an hour... with or without us.

"*Khagas tsag!*" the driver's assistant reasserted to Vinko as we passed by, pointing at his watch.

"You really are a bastard," Vinko said in English, saluting him.

I spent most of the rest stop leaning against a delguur wall, stomping my feet on the ground to keep them warm, smoking a cigarette and feeding delguur cookies to stray dogs. While I engaged in micro-charity, Vinko went to get a drink of vodka at the nearest gwanz. He emerged a few minutes later, and came and leaned on the wall next to me.

"You shouldn't feed them, you know," he said after a while, watching me as I tossed cookies to the gathering crowd of pitiful canines.

"What, these poor guys?" I asked, handing a cookie to a crippled mutt on my left. "Why not?"

"First of all, they're probably infested with diseases," Vinko said, scrunching his face at the mangy mess eating from my hand. "You know what kinds of horrors those things eat? Man, on my last supply run to U.B., I saw this one gwanz dog eat maggots from its own festering flesh wound... just slurped them up like little clumps of rice. Think about that the next time you let one of these 'poor guys' lick cookies from your hand."

"The Corps gave us, like, twelve different kinds of vaccinations, man," I said. "It's all good."

"Second of all," Vinko continued, "giving food to these stray dogs provides them an artificial nutrition source that contributes to overpopulation. The longer stray dogs live, the longer they have sex. The longer they have sex, the more puppies they have. And then you have three dozen more starving puppies on your hands. All because you feel too guilty to let one of them die."

I laughed. "Vinko, man, you'd make a great nature show host... you know that? I'm just feeding some dogs, that's all."

He shrugged, and I continued to distribute cookies to the dogs for a few minutes until I ran out.

"Sorry fuckers," I said to the pitiful mass of mutt-hounds before me, waving the empty bag in the air. "Good luck to you all."

I went inside the closest delguur and threw the bag in the trash. When I came out, Vinko was smoking a cigarette and waving the dogs away. The poor beasts had scattered like billiards struck by a cue ball.

Vinko handed me a cigarette. I took it and resumed leaning against the delguur wall.

"We've got them in Baganolgii too," Vinko said after a moment.

"What's that?" I said.

"Stray dogs, I mean... tons of them, man."

"Mmmm hmmm."

"You can hear them barking all night. They're out in the steppe, they're in the village, they're in the *hashaa* alleyways. Sometimes they run in packs, dozens of them, fighting in the night over scraps of meat and garbage."

I nodded. "We've got them in Mandalzuud too. Where do you think they come from?"

"Who knows?" Vinko said, throwing up his hands.

We stood there for a minute, breathing in smoke. Minutes passed before Vinko spoke again.

"You probably think that I'm an asshole, huh?" he said, his voice stuttering with a sudden vulnerability. "Because of the dogs, I mean."

"Nah," I said.

"You know how they deal with the stray dog problem in Baganolgii?" Vinko continued.

"How?"

"Once a year, the village government organizes a village-wide dog hunt, offering a thousand tugrug bounty for each dog carcass. On that day, anyone looking to make a few bucks leaves the house with whatever weapons they can find... carbine rifles, bows and arrows, sharpened sticks... and then they go out looking for stray dogs. At the end of the day, they turn in their kills to the village government, which officially tallies them and makes the cash payouts. They call it 'The Hunt'... some look forward to it all year."

I raised an eyebrow. "You're kidding me."

Vinko chuckled. "Who'd make something like that up? They'd have to be sick in the head."

"What the hell do they do with all those dead dogs, then?"

"Some guy with a flatbed truck comes and they load it up with all the carcasses. Then they drive a few kilometers out into the steppe and dump the bodies in the khuudo, and set the heap on fire so that the dogs that escaped the cull can't feed off the dead ones."

"Jesus," I said.

Before Vinko could respond, a terrifying honk came from our bus, signifying that we had about a minute to make it onboard before the driver left us in Gwanztown for good. We dashed for the bus, making it with moments to spare, hopping aboard as the driver's assistant gave us a dirty look.

"Dead dogs dumped in the steppe," I muttered loudly as we maneuvered down the aisle towards the Puke Seat. "What a goddamn place to live."

"Well, that's Mongolia," Vinko said, as we plopped down in our seats. "Would it be more humane to take them to a concrete cell and give them lethal injections? They're just doing what they have to do."

And I was silent then. I had read and heard these exact words - THEY'RE JUST DOING WHAT THEY HAVE TO DO – used to justify a million horrors, a million war crimes, a million misdeeds borne from greed or turpitude or survival instinct, all vastly crueler than a few hundred dead dogs in the steppe. But something about the phrase stuck with me this time, and I couldn't get it out of my head. As the bus started up with a roar and sped away from Gwanztown, I leaned my head against the window and pondered the words...

They're just doing what they have to do.

And for an hour, I said nothing.

After a while, Vinko must have seen that gears were turning in my head. "What's the matter with you?" he eventually asked, looking up from his ipod and raising an eyebrow.

But I had no clue what to tell him. What could I say? That I was beginning to think that Ralph might have been on to something all those months ago in Delgerkhovd... and maybe... just maybe... "everything *was* the same everywhere?" What if the human condition is exactly that - the *human* condition - and life *everywhere* is absurd and cruel? What if we're all rats in a maze which has no ending, no cheese, only death and sorrow and monotony and desperation, everywhere struggle, everywhere craziness, no true meaning to all of our desperate labors, forever doomed to be "doing what we have to do", be it working in a cubicle for forty years or scooping dead dogs onto the back of a pickup truck?

But how can you tell people such things?

How can you dare believe them yourself?

"Nothing," I finally said. "Nothing's wrong at all, dude."

We sat there for a minute in silence, my last words echoing in the stale air of the overcrowded bus. For a minute, I thought that the conversation was over. Then, very slowly, Vinko put his ipod in his coat pocket, laid his head back on the seat and stared up at the roof. A long Gobi second passed before he spoke.

"You know," he said at last, "I volunteered to carry the bodies."

I stared at him. "What?"

He continued to stare at the roof of the bus. "The stray dogs that they killed in my village. I helped them lift those bloody dog carcasses into the flatbed truck, then I drove out to the khuudo with them and dumped the bodies in a gully. I was part of the whole goddamn thing. I helped them to organize the hunt, print flyers... hell... I even bought them a tank of gas out of my own pocket. And I *volunteered* for it all."

"What the fuck, man, why would you do that?"

He swung his head to the side to look at me. "Each of those dog carcasses was worth 1,000 tugrugs. Think about that, man. A thousand... stinking... tugrugs... each. Those hunters made in one day what they normally make in three months."

"Yeah," I said, "and I'll bet you that half of them went out and spent it on vodka and cigarettes."

"Yeah... half did. But half of them didn't. Half of them used the money to put food on the table for their families, or buy schoolbooks for their kids, or to restock the coal bin. Those dog corpses did a lot of good for our village, and although I hate to say it, they ended up being unimaginably more valuable dead than alive. Look man, it's not like I don't like dogs... I love dogs. In fact, the whole hunt is disgusting, from the event itself to the people running it. But I tried my best to make it a success anyway, because that's what I'm here to do. That's what put bread on the goddamn table. And I'm not saying that I'm some sort of better person for it, because I know that I'm not. But if we pick and choose who and how we help in this fucked up world, a lot of people are going to fall through the cracks. Ethics have killed more people than bubonic plague and the automobile combined, and I'm sick of being their bitch."

Vinko stopped for a moment and looked at me. Despite the feigned calm on his face, his eyes seemed desperate, like a beached jellyfish pleading not to be poked with a stick. I immediately recognized the look... it was the same one I had been staring at in the mirror for the past year. We were both catching sight of some faraway sight on the horizon, a terrible secret that nobody else could see, a tiny plume of factory smoke hidden amongst a sky full of feathery clouds.

And we both were beginning to smell something rotten with this whole "Saving the World" gig.

"I just want it to all make sense again," Vinko said after a while. "You know what I mean?"

"Hell... maybe it's not supposed to make sense," I said.

Vinko shook his head. "No..." he protested weakly, sounding more like he was trying to convince himself than me. "There's something more to it all... I'm sure of it, man. There's a plan... there's a goddamn plan... and it includes all of this... even the dead dogs."

"How can you be so sure?" I asked.

"I wasn't going to mention this," he said, "because I know that it sounds a little crazy. But you've lived in the Gobi as long as I have now, and if there's anyone that will understand what I'm going to say, you will."

Vinko looked around the bus conspiratorially, waiting until he was sure that nobody was listening before continuing. "Have you ever heard of the Mongolian Death Worm?"

I thought back to the time when I had first read about the *Allgkhoi Khorkhoy*... the mythical, giant, killer worm of the deep Gobi Desert... the beast that could whip electricity like an eel and had acid for saliva... the most feared and cryptic predator of them all. I thought about how I had laughed then, like I would have laughed at the mention of Bigfoot or the Loch Ness Monster. But then I remembered my past months in Mandalzuud.

And suddenly, the existence of something like the Death Worm didn't seem so crazy after all.

"Yeah," I admitted. "I've heard about it."

Vinko's eyes bulged. "Well, the next time you're walking alone in the desert at night, do me a favor and listen extra carefully. The next time that you see a shadow shift, wait an extra second before you turn your head. And the next time that you feel like there's something watching you... somewhere out in the darkness... somewhere closer than you realize... think about what I'm telling you now."

"What's that?" I asked.

Vinko smiled. "Maybe... just maybe... there might be a God after all."

And the bus continued on through the endless steppe of the Gobi.

~ 14 ~

The Singing Sands

When I returned from Ulaanbaatar, the water jug in my ger was only *half* frozen.

And I couldn't have been happier.

The most brutal winter I had ever known was receding, like a stubborn ocean wave or the fading glimmer in the eye of a freshly-slaughtered goat. The killer chill of the winter wind was beginning to lose its edge, the thermometer was heading back into the positives, and all the Gobi was singing with the news.

As the land thawed out, the sickly-rich scent of melting sod settled on the steppe like a wet blanket. The first birds began to return a few weeks later... frail, dusty-grey Gobi larks... migrating home to the desert from the east... reveling in the brief respite before the hawks and vultures arrived. Out in the khuudo, the herders began to unbundle the blankets that they'd wrapped around their cattle all winter to keep them from freezing. In the village, the ger dwellers began to "de-winterize" their homes, unwrapping the thick, winter layers of felt from their gers, like they were peeling giant, boiled eggs. Soot was banged from stovepipes. Rugs were hung and swatted. Outdoor sex once again became a possibility.

And then one beautiful day in early March, we got rain.

It began early that evening, when the sky was still a deep, booming purple, the beautiful zen of the moment striking me mute. By the time night fell, the rain had quickened its pace exponentially, like a jogger descending a sudden steep slope. I laid in bed for hours that night, listening entranced to the thousand voices of the rainfall...

DRUPPP - droplets falling on the canvas of my ger.

TLINK TINK - plummeting water beads on the window-panes.

SSSSZZZZZZZ - evaporating sizzles on the scorching stovepipe.

As the first rain of the season swooshed over the steppe, my fellow villagers began to lose themselves in the ecstasy of the springtime Gobi, undergoing a series of subtle, bio-chemical adjustments that sharpened their senses. Indeed, the rural Mongolian is much more aligned to seasonal patterns than an average American. It is something ingrained in their blood, like their ability to instinctively know what compass point they are facing (human tuning forks, every one of them). And all around me, my Mandalzuud neighbors were changing their daily patterns with the coming spring, ebbing and flowing with the Earth as most Americans ebb and flow around a time-clock.

It was a behavior that I tried to mimic the best I could. But ever since returning from PDM, I had been operating on some different inner temporal sense, a strange and possibly broken chronometer, not wholly Mongolian or American. It was a warped sense of time, no longer living according to days or weeks or seasons or zones, perched like a spider in an hourglass. There was a terrible sense of urgency that wrecked any shred of daily zen I had left… impatience washing dishes, impatience making lesson plans, impatience wiping my ass.

The only thing that centered me in any sort of fixed time was the radio station. We had sent our grant proposal to USAID a week after the PDM seminar, but I still hadn't got so much as a courtesy call from the funding committee. In the meanwhile, the thought of the station was consuming me like syphilis, eating up all of my sanity and spare time. It was like I had eaten a sharp sliver of broken mirror and was being sliced up from the inside out. At night, instead of playing my guitar or writing poetry, I would stay up late drinking vodka and making lists of things that I needed to do for the station. I would wake up in the middle of the night, freezing and shivering at my desk, pen in hand and a plethora of indecipherable lists rustling together like steel chains in my fevered imagination.

And I began to lose it.

My neighbors, Purevdorj and Khishigtuul, had noticed that I had been keeping strange hours. How could they not… after midnight, my ger was often the only one with its lights on for a quarter mile in any direction.

"They think that you are lonesome," Tsetseg confided to me one Sunday, over tea.

"Huh?" I asked, surprised. "Why didn't they tell me so?"

"They think it will make you... shy... if they say so. It is not the Mongol way to say these things. We think that it is very sad for someone to be alone, for any reason."

"I'm just trying to get a little work done," I said defensively, taking a swig of my tea. "I'm fine. Really. Thanks for asking."

Tsetseg looked me over tenderly, like a mother penguin examining an egg for cracks. Finally after a moment, apparently satisfied, she nodded and picked up a biscuit to nibble on.

"*Zuger*," she said, "We all must work."

***

Shortly after the first springtime rain, sandstorm season arrived in Mandalzuud.

The gusts of the Gobi were always strong, but they began to bluster up even more in early April. The winds sent every particle of sand and topsoil into perpetual motion, leaping and tumbling after themselves like lions after a gazelle. During the first days of the sandstorm season, the effect was exquisite, psychedelic, as if there were hidden elves and fairies behind every gain of sand.

But as I learned during my first Mongol winter, such things are always beautiful at first.

By the end of the month, the winds had turned uncontrollably savage. They gnawed and gnashed at anything that wasn't tied down securely, like a billion invisible teeth chattering day and night, knocking the cherry out of my cigarette and blowing piss in my face whenever I was careless enough to urinate outside facing the wrong direction. The Gobi winds would puff massive cyclones of sand and dust into the air in rusty-colored bursts, which roared down the hashaa alleyways with the ferocity of demons, blasting the paint off fences and sending hashaa dogs running for cover.

And still, we had not seen the worst of it.

In May, the winds peaked at a feverish pace, fracturing and bending with violent whip strokes across the steppe. The gales blew thick curtains of sand skyward, deep as San Francisco fog, darkening the sky with a Biblical vigor. When the sands took to the air, travel slowed to a crawl - nobody could see where they were driving - and a trip to Ulaanbaatar might take days if one got caught in a prolonged sandstorm. During these periods, people would struggle through the village the best they could, garbed in secondhand biker goggles and head scarves, like extras meandering around the set of a Mad Max movie. Soon, as the frayed and winter-worn cables connecting Mandalzuud to the national power grid began to snap, village-wide power outages began to hit. The blackouts would come a few hours into a wind storm, snuffing out the few electric comforts we had, leaving the village breathless until the break was found and fixed sometime in the next day or two.

By the end of the month, the power outages were coming once a week and lasting for days on end.

Whenever the sandstorms came, Mandalzuud was a bleak desert world, some inhospitable and apocalyptic sand planet from Dune or Star Wars. Outside, sand particles crashed against each other in the wind, making ghostly moans whole locations I could never quite pinpoint. Occasionally a massive swirling tempest of sand and silt would blot out the afternoon sun like an eclipse, and everything would turn to night until the storm passed.

Purevdorj and Khishigtuul had helped me to prepare my ger for sandstorm season a few weeks before it arrived, but despite the extra moorings and ropes, my home took the full brunt of the desert maelstroms. The unforgiving winds pummeled my suddenly-tiny tent, producing terrifying creaking noises as the wooden framework supporting the roof over my head struggled to maintain its grip. As it did, a fine dust would blow through the innumerable cracks and spaces in my ger walls - even coming down my stovepipe - coating everything in the ger with a layer of Gobi silt. At night I would lay awake as the gales buffeted my tent, listening as they beat against the felt walls like horny phantoms trying to get in and rape me. I lay there silently on my plank bed, watching the wooden skeleton of the ger heave in and out rhythmically like the ribcage of some enormous animal, wondering if *this was the night* that two thousand years of Mongolian architectural evolution was going to fail, and the whole wretched structure was going to crash down on my head and squash me like a bug.

But the night never came.

***

"Are the sandstorms always this bad in Mandalzuud?" I asked Tsetseg one Sunday at tea.

My counterpart only shrugged. To her and most other Mongols, weather could never be "good" or "bad"... it could only *be*.

"Many old men and women in Mandalzuud say that the sandstorms are getting worse," she said at last, more to be polite than to give me an answer. "They say that many years ago, the Gobi was much quieter."

"But what do *you* think," I asked.

Tsetseg sat for a second, taking a few tentative sips from her teacup. "You will laugh," she said.

"Of course not," I told her.

"Americans *always* laugh at Mongol explanations."

"Not this time," I said.

"*Zuger*. I will tell you what I think... the desert is angry."

"The desert is angry," I repeated, trying not to sound incredulous.

Tsetseg nodded. "When my mother was a girl, before she came to Mandalzuud, she lived in very south Gobi near the *Khongoryn Els*... the Singing Sands, I think Americans call this place. In the Khongoryn Els, the sand is very special, very round. When the wind blows in the right way, sometimes the sand of Khongoryn Els can make a special noise, like a music note. When I was young, my mother told me stories about the singing sand. Sometimes she would cry when she talked about the sounds they made."

"What sort of sounds?" I asked.

Tsetseg closed her eyes for a moment, conjuring some far lost memory in her mind. "Each time, I would ask my mother that question. And each time, she told me the same answer."

Tsetseg opened her eyes, grabbed for her English-Mongol dictionary off her desk, and flipped through the pages for a minute. She squinted and pointed at a word, then turned the book to me. "How do you say this?"

I looked to where she was pointing. "Lullaby," I pronounced.

She nodded. "Lull-a-bye... that is what she called it. The Gobi was making lull-a-bye for the people of the khuudo. "

Tsetseg laid her dictionary back down and looked out the window. The next words out of her mouth were spoken softly, with a tinge of guilt.

"The old people of Mandalzuud used to say that sometimes, the sand would make the same song here. In the old days, they say, the people lived as part of the land, and the Gobi was happy to have them. They were mother and child with the sands, and everything was 'fair', as you always say. But now the old ones say that young Mongolians are forgetting how to live with the Gobi, and the sand is not singing anymore. It is not singing because it is angry. It is quiet because we are not family anymore."

Tsetseg sat back in her chair. "You say that you listen to the sand as well, true?"

I nodded.

"And what does it sound like to you?" she asked.

I looked at her for a moment in consternation, trying to decide what to say. I knew what she expected me to tell her, that the whole idea of the singing sand was crazy... that it was only a natural scientific phenomenon of peculiarly shaped sand. But for some reason, I couldn't bring myself to say the words. Maybe it was because I really wanted to believe that sands could sing, not like an American would "believe", but like a Mongolian would.

There is something really important here, I thought, *some concept that I've been searching for... something that I need to understand.... some kind of deep, mother fucking magic.*

But no matter how I tried, I couldn't make myself feel something that wasn't there. And the truth was, when I listened to the sounds of the sands, all I could hear was dissonance - not anger or peace or zen - only the random unmeaning of babbling sand particles.

Just like holding a gun to your head.

"It sounds lonely," I finally said, answering her question. "Goddamn lonely."

And we sat there and finished our tea in silence.

$$\sim 15 \sim$$

<u>Soggtoes</u>

The post-sandstorm Gobi spring is a beautiful time and place to know. The days are long, the temperatures calm and nurturing, and the skies are a deeper shade of blue than the human mind can imagine. Life teems at every turn, love rides sweet on the winds of the steppe, and waking dreams float about the land, thick as pie aroma.

But with the spring also comes the *soggtoes*.

A soggtoe - the Mongolian term for a chronic drunk - is perhaps the lowest form of human in Mongolia. Mostly composed of sad, lost and habitually unemployable men, the soggtoe population is a melancholy reminder of what happens when human beings lose hope. Habitual line-steppers, soggtoes exist on a diet of cheap Xaraa vodka and broken promises. Their breath is fetid and gangrenous, their dels are tattered from being dragged in the dust and shit, their faces are eternally swollen and sweaty, and their dispositions are among the worst on Earth. In the spring, the soggtoes emerge in swarms like locusts woken from a deep winter's hibernation... terrible, migrating wild men loosed to wreak havoc on their brethren.... puking, slurring and mumbling in a cryptic language that bears only a vague resemblance to Mongolian.

The closest relative of the soggtoe in America is the crackhead, but even crackheads can be reasoned with, if only with the threat of brute force. There is no such respite with a soggtoe. The proper way to treat one of these creatures is as if they were a child on LSD, wielding a Bowie knife. Soggtoes retain no rational thought processes, and cannot be bargained with, pacified or otherwise bought off. They are not men, anymore. They are ciphers... forces of nature... demons... and there's a hell of a lot of them these days.

My duty as an American - and a Peace Corps volunteer - was to tolerate these forces of nature, as one tolerates monsoon season or the occasional earthquake.

But there's only so much that a person can take.

***

It was a Thursday afternoon, and I was on my way to the post office to mail a letter, when I almost got myself kicked out of the Peace Corps.

I was taking the long way, through a seldom used stretch of steppe on the edge of the village, and the day was clear as baby's breath. Sometimes the beauty of springtime Gobi steals your mind, and if I was paying more attention, I might have noticed the dread scent of soggtoe in the air, creeping along my skin like a gossamer spider.

But I didn't... and there he was.

The soggtoe was sitting cross-legged on the ground among the weed bushes and steppe-grass when I passed him, dressed in a dirty jean jacket and a pair of crusty sweat pants, mumbling to himself and rubbing a hand through his stubbly hair. About thirty years old, the soggtoe's face was already a well-folded map of wrinkles and creases. I could immediately tell that he had been up for at least a few days - or was batshit insane - because of the way that his unfocused eyes rolled in their sockets.

I had never seen the man before, which meant that he was most likely from the khuudo. I had learned that this was something to beware; like Rumplestiltskin of legend, soggtoes lose much of their power if you can call them by name. Subtly, I corrected my walking trajectory, as one would adjust their path to avoid a rattlesnake.

Jesus God, I thought, increasing my pace.

But it was too late. As I crept past, the soggtoe suddenly snapped to attention, as if he had been awakened by the snapping of a twig. I could feel the soggtoes' eyes following me, like some sort of drunken reptile sighting his prey before the kill. With an immense amount of willpower, the soggtoe struggled to his feet. His mouth opened to form words.

"HOOOOOOEEEEEEEEY!" he yelled after me in a guttural mishmash, like a zombie shouting for *BRAAAAAAIIINNNNNSSS.*

I doubled my stride.

"HOOOOOOEEEEEEEEY!" the soggtoe shouted again, this time louder and more garbled. He began to follow me, dragging his feet through the dirt as he tried his best to keep up.

"*HOOOOOOEEEEEEEY!*" he continued to shout, waving his hands.

And so it continued until I reached the post office. As I arrived, I paused outside to stub out my cigarette in the dirt. I could still hear the soggtoe coming, bellowing inanities as he sloppily pressed onward, and I knew that eventually he would catch up to me... there were only so many places I could go. And if I went into the post office, he would surely be waiting for me outside when I was done. Maybe he'd even follow me inside and cause a scene.

Anyway, I thought. *What the hell is this? I'm a goddamn United States Peace Corps volunteer... more importantly, I'm from New Jersey... and I don't have to take this shit!*

Leaning against a metal hitching post in front of the post office, I waited as my new friend caught up. When he saw that I was waiting, the soggtoe began to take his time stumbling after me, which gave me plenty of time to stand there and get progressively more pissed off. By the time he came within shouting distance, I was dangerously livid with bravado.

"*Yu? Chinni ner khen be? Yu heej been ve?*" I demanded, as the soggtoe closed the gap between us. "What the Chrissakes do you want?"

The soggtoe staggered up to me, wearing the grin of an old college drinking buddy about to hit a fraternity brother up for a free beer. He spoke in rapid, bumblebee Mongolian that I couldn't quite understand, punctuating his speech with ambiguous hand gestures.

"I can't understand you... *oilgogkhgui!*" I objected after a minute or so, looking around fruitlessly for any witnesses or bystanders who could take this freak off my hands.

The soggtoe maneuvered his way in front of me and continued to bark in rapid-fire Mongolian, slurring his words together like porridge and flailing his arms around wildly like a Muppet. As he jabbered, flecks of spittle sprayed from his mouth and landed on my shirt, and he kept inching closer to me until our knees were almost touching. All the while, the soggtoe kept trying to put his hand on my shoulder, but each time he did I would shrug it off. And each time I did, he began to get a little more enraged.

Finally, I could take no more.

"Look here, you goddamn mook!" I emphasized slightly louder than I intended, pointing at an imaginary watch on my wrist. "I'm very busy... *zavgui*... do you understand? You need to get to the goddamn point and quick. *Yu heej been ve?*"

Perhaps sensing that the time had come to make his move, the soggtoe outstretched his arm and held out his hand in the universal gesture.

"*Muung,*" he said, finality in his voice.

"Money," I echoed, not believing what I was hearing.

"*Muung,*" the soggtoe repeated, sticking his hand in my face.

"Goldfish and pussy lips... you're twisted in the head!" I exclaimed, amazed at his audacity. "You're not getting one tugrug from me, you goddamn crook!"

Turning my back to him, I prepared to walk away. I should have known better... Traveler's rule number 1: Never turn your back on a drunk when you're in a foreign land. Before I could leave, the soggtoe grabbed me by the jacket with his greasy fingers, pulling me back towards him. My first instinct was to immediately lash out with a donkey kick and strike to cripple, but instead I held myself in check and simply tried to twist loose from the drunk's grasp. But the bastard's grip was strong with thirty summer's worth of digging, and though his feet wobbled under him, he hung on to my shirt firmly, jabbering at me all the while in sloppy Mongolian.

"What the fuck!" I yelled, unconsciously balling up my fists despite myself. "Do you know who I am? Get off of me you fucking lush, or there's going to be trouble!"

I spun around, finally twisting myself free from his grip. But the soggtoe immediately recovered and closed in on me again, holding out an outstretched palm.

"*Muung!*" he slurred insistently. "*Muung!*"

I briefly thought back to all the countless times in America that I'd given money to bums, panhandlers, street musicians and buskers, never thinking twice about it or caring if they spent the money on booze or drugs. But this was different, some sort of hostile encounter that bordered on robbery, and there was no chance this guy was getting a single tugrug.

And in my fractured Mongolian, I told him exactly that.

I'm not sure if the soggtoe understood the letter of my speech, but its meaning was definitely clear. He withdrew his hand, and I could almost see the diseased thoughts rumbling through his intoxicated head. He took half a step back.

And then, very slowly and deliberately, the bastard stepped on one of my shoes.

I was shocked. To a Mongolian, this was the ultimate challenge, the equivalent of "Fuck your momma" in America. And it was then that I knew we were going to have to settle this, one way or another. It was at that exact moment of pending truth that both of us heard a rumble in the distance. I looked up to see a motorcycle bearing down on us... Batchuluun, the lone village police officer on duty that day.

As Batchuluun roared towards us, I could see that he had an empty jerry can on the back of his bike, and had probably been on his way to fetch water when he saw the soggtoe and I grappling. Whatever the reason, I knew that his arrival was a one-in-a-thousand chance.

Finally ...a goddamn break, I thought.

"*Hoooeyyy... tsagdaa!*" I yelled out, waving.

As Batchuluun pulled up beside us and got off his cycle, the soggtoe took a step back from me. The cop was larger than both of us, a barrel-chested, Ghengis of a Mongol, and there was no question that he could mop up the desert floor with both of us if he so desired.

"*Yarcen ve?*" Batchuluun asked politely but with authority, clearly speaking to me, yet keeping eye contact with the soggtoe the entire time.

As I attempted to explain what happened in my feeble Mongolian, the soggtoe began to blubber to Batchuluun in a cowed voice, trying feebly to contradict my version of the story. Interrupted from my train of thought, I bristled with indignity, preparing to demand that I be heard out. But I needn't have worried. Before I knew it, Batchuluun's massive hand struck out like lightning, crashing into the soggtoe's gut like a grizzly bear paw. I watched the soggtoe recoil from the blow, his eyes bulging from the sudden impact, his body crumpling as the air rushed out of his diaphragm. He began to make weird little inhaling noises, like he was trying to suck up the last bit of soda with a straw.

"Wait to speak," Batchuluun cautioned the soggtoe in Mongolian, speaking in a calm tone that was somehow more menacing than if he had yelled. When the soggtoe had ceased his blubbering, Batchuluun looked at me politely and nodded for me to finish.

"Ummm... that's it," I said, shrugging, suddenly feeling uneasy that I had drug the cops into this. "*Muung ogcengui.*"

Batchuluun chortled. Then, turning to the soggtoe, he began his interrogation. It lasted about ten seconds. All he asked was one question...

"Did you drink vodka?"

The soggtoe just nodded, his eyes full of fear.

That was all Batchuluun needed. Without any further hesitation, the cop grabbed the drunk and swung him to his feet. The soggtoe whimpered and tried his best to keep up, as Batchuluun half-dragged him over to a metal railing near the side of the post office. As I followed along, not sure what to do, Batchuluun sat the soggtoe down on the ground near the railing and pulled out a set of handcuffs.

"What are you going to do with those?" I asked in Mongolian, staring at the cuffs.

Batchuluun smiled. "Mongol prison," he deadpanned, and then he fastened the soggtoe's wrist to the railing. As the handcuffs clicked shut, the soggtoe moaned softly in a weak protest and began to clink the cuffs against the railing, but after a harsh look from the cop he stopped and lay still, his arm twisted slightly as if he were patting himself on the back.

When he was done, Batchuluun leaned down to the soggtoe and told him that he would be back to let him loose at nightfall. And then with a quick salute to me, he turned to get back on his motorcycle.

"Wait," I said in Mongolian, pointing down at the dejected and defeated soggtoe. "You're just going to leave him there?"

Batchuluun nodded.

"But... you can't do that!" I protested.

"Why not?" he asked, genuinely confused.

And then it dawned on me how silly I must have sounded.

"Nevermind," I said after a moment. "Thank you."

After one more quick salute to me and a glance at the immobile soggtoe, Batchuluun started up his cycle and was gone, and I was left staring blankly at the pathetic wretch that lay shackled to the railing before me. Now that Batchuluun was gone, the soggtoe began to struggle against his handcuffs again. But all the fight had gone out of him, and the best he could manage was a weak clunking motion of the wrist. As it became apparent that he was stuck for good, the soggtoe began to let out a terrible moan, a deep ululation that echoed far into the distance.

I stared down at the soggtoe and watched him struggle. Only a few minutes before, I had been one iota away from punching him in the face. Now the fucker was completely at my mercy. I looked around; despite the hullabaloo and the continued wailing of the soggtoe, there were no villagers in sight.

No witnesses.

But as I gazed down at the soggtoe, the anger drained from my soul like spaghetti water through a sieve. This is still a human being, I realized. And as I watched the soggtoe broken-heartedly struggle against his handcuffs, the truth hit me like a yo-yo in the balls.

This was who I was here to save in the first place.

I had come to Mongolia to heal the lepers and clothe the naked... to be the martyr that the downtrodden and hopeless of the world needed and deserved. But here before me was the very victim I had sought, and instead of redemption, all I could see was a wretched, despicable mess.

Was it so long ago that I was the savior of all mankind? I asked myself.

Down on the ground, the soggtoe was looking up at me with a sorrowful cut to his face. He continued to moan, using the full weight of his dead body to lean against the handcuffs, like an animal in a bear trap trying to gnaw its own foot off. And in that moment, he became a symbol for something larger... some terrible despair that I could never truly heal or even understand... an ancient malaise that was larger than the sum of all the ethnicities, nations, religions or classes of the world... a condition that has existed before America, before Mongolia, and even before civilization itself.

In that moment, for the briefest of instants, I understood him.

And without further ado, I left him there, chained to the railing and moaning.

~ 16 ~

<u>The Caveat</u>

On June 3, I got a wakeup call from the village post master, Gombosuren.

"Air-Eek-Bagsh-aaaaaaaaahhhhhhhhhh! Where have you been?" Gombo hollered to me in Mongolian from across my hashaa, beeping his motorcycle horn until I came outside. "There was a phone call for you at the post office two hours ago!"

Such was my voicemail system in those days.

When I arrived at the post office, Gombo handed me a scrap of paper with a phone number scrawled on it.

"Do you know who they are?" I asked in Mongolian. "What did they want?"

Gombo shrugged. "They spoke English."

"OK then... let's give 'em a call Gombo," I answered, handing him the paper back and nodding. "*Yarekh, yarekh, yarekh.*"

The postman took the paper back and dialed in the numbers on the ancient rotary phone. When the phone began to ring, he reached over the counter and handed me the receiver. I took it and nodded gratefully.

The line rang twice more before a woman's voice picked up.

"Rebecca Hohn... USAID," she said, leaving a pause for me to identify myself.

"Eric Kiefer... Peace Corps volunteer in Mandalzuud, Dundgobi," I replied, feeling as if I was in the military. "Someone here called me?"

"Ah... Eric," the woman said, taking a deep breath. I listened to her shift around some papers. "Yes, I tried to get in touch with you this morning. USAID has received and reviewed your application for a SPA grant... I think it was to build a radio station, right?"

"Right!" I interjected, a little too eagerly.

"Well, I've got some good news," she told me. "Your grant application has been approved. The full amount of $4,000 will be deposited into an account in your name at the Trade and Development Bank in Ulaanbaatar in one week."

And just like that, the money was ours.

***

The very next weekend, Tsetseg and I took the grueling bus trip to Ulaanbaatar to pick up our money and buy our radio equipment.

Although it felt strange to admit it, I was goddamn thrilled to go shopping. Our spree wasn't the normal American consumer frenzy, but something pure, something we were doing to tilt the scales in favor of good. My dream of a radio station was finally taking some sort of physical form, becoming something that I could touch with my hands.

Finally, I thought... *a chance to prove I'm not a crummy human being.*

From the State Department store, we got a brand new, rack mounted CD and VCD player. From the Flower Center shopping co-op, we got some microphones and an 8-channel mixer. From the massive open-air bazaar on the east out-skirts of the city – what the locals call the *Kharr Zakh* (The Black Market) - we got everything else... paint, office sup-plies, brooms, brushes and enough assorted music to fill a year's worth of air time.

My next move was to call Alexei. To my surprise, the Russian remembered who I was almost immediately.

"Do you have real money?" were the first words out of his mouth.

"How does $2,500 American dollars sound?" I replied.

The following day, Tsetseg and I took a taxi to the address that Alexei had given us. The dusty, little shop was located on the fringe of the city - in the old district - where the signs were still written in old Mongolian and the denizens still dis-trusted Americans. When Tsetseg and I walked into the store, a large and calloused Russian was sitting at a desk behind the front counter. He was dressed in a business-style leisure suit, his feet tipped up on a cinder block, his face hidden behind a huge Cossack beard, looking neither mean nor obstinate... only impassive.

"Alexei?" I asked, stepping up to shake his hand.

The man smiled, shaking Tsetseg's hand in turn. "I am so. And you must be American who needs radio transmitter. Welcome to my shop."

His English had improved tremendously since the last time we had spoken and I told him so. Alexei dismissed my compliment with a wave. "Ah well... I have been practicing. It is not every day I talk with Americans... or Mongols who speak English. Please come."

We followed him to the back room of the shop, which was filled with tables with dozens of radio transmitters, antennas and unrecognizable electronic gear in various stages of completion... an electronics apothecary. When he reached a metal case about the size of a microwave, Alexei stopped.

"This is your transmitter," he said, tapping on the box's metal casing. He motioned to a lamp-sized satellite dish next to it. "And this is antenna. And here is cable... it goes here and here."

As Alexei pointed, I looked down at the pile of equipment on the table. It didn't seem like much. But I knew that this simple-looking pile of wires and chips was capable of more violence and terror than a hundred atom bombs.

"Did you bring money?" Alexei asked.

Tsetseg stepped forward and took our wad of cash - freshly withdrawn from the bank that morning - from out of its hiding place in her sock. Alexei took the money from her with a smile, and leaned back against the wall to count. When he was satisfied, he wadded the roll up in his fist and put it in his pocket.

"Equipment is now yours," he said, flashing us a toothy smile. "If I may ask one question."

I looked over at Tsetseg. She shrugged.

"What do you want to know?" I told Alexei.

His hands folded together in a little steeple. "Why do you build this radio station in the Gobi?"

Taking a deep breath, I launched into my speech about village needs and sustainability, the same rehearsed claptrap that I had spoon fed to USAID to swindle them out of their money. But Alexei stopped me almost immediately, shaking his head like a chess grandmaster criticizing a student's move.

"No, no…" he said. "You misunderstand my words. I must know why YOU build radio station."

"Me?" I asked.

Alexei nodded.

"Why does it matter?" I asked, trying to dodge the question.

"The tools I give you are very powerful. Men use these things to do much evil. I must know who uses my equipment," the Russian said, not budging. "Is your answer so hard to explain?"

"Not at all," I said loudly, not knowing why it *was*.

"Then why do you make this radio station?"

"Because I'm trying to save the world!" I exclaimed suddenly, shocked by how silly the words sounded. "OK? I'm trying to save the world, Alexei! Is that what you want to hear?"

I stood there silently fuming, not knowing why the Russian's prodding had affected me so badly. It was a moment before I noticed that Alexei wasn't looking at me, but at my counterpart... Tsetseg... standing off to the side of us, her hands in her pockets, her eyes cast downward at the floor. And that's when I realized that this was the first time my counterpart had ever heard my true reason for being in Mongolia.

It was the first time she learned that I was trying to "save" her.

Alexei watched us for a moment, his eyes searching for the answers that none of us were willing to speak. "You want to save the world, eh?"

I said nothing.

"So it is," Alexei said at last, waving his hand dismissively. He had heard what he wanted. "It is good enough. You can have equipment. But I must warn you..."

"I know about electrical safety," I interrupted. "Don't worry about..."

"This is not warning for transmitter," Alexei continued, giving me a sharp look. "This is warning for *you*. I have been living in Mongolia for twenty years now, American, and you are not the first of your kind I have seen. You come to buy a transmitter, but you have no money. You come seeking freedom, but not a key. And you come to *save the world*, but you do not come to love it... Do you understand?"

"Not at all," I admitted. "But thanks for the warning."

Alexei sighed and nodded. "*Dosvydania*, American. I hope it serves you well."

<u>Lemons for Lemonade</u>

As soon as Tsetseg and I were back in Mandalzuud, work on our radio station commenced.

It would not prove to be as easy as I had hoped.

Located in the attic of the post office, dusty and forgotten by the years, accessible only by a narrow and treacherous staircase, the room that Boldbaatar had promised us for our radio station – the "Ghost Room" - was essentially a skeleton. The first time that I saw it, I thought that I had wandered into a tomb. Mausoleum petite and torture-room chic, the room had the ambiance of a prison cell. The walls were scarred with age and weather, the arid air of the Gobi accelerating the decay by decades. Some bastard had thrown a rock through the room's only window, and the jagged remains of the window pane had been clumsily boarded over with a single rotting piece of plywood. Every surface area within view was caked with a thick layer of dust and mold, and thick festoons of cobwebs clung tenaciously to every corner and nook, like vines in a jungle. There was no electricity (or even outlets), and no furniture, except for a useless garbage heap of broken office chairs in one corner. There was also no insulation or ventilation, and I knew that the room would be like the rest of Mandalzuud... deadly freezing in the winter and stifling as wool underpants in the summer.

But it was *ours*, and that was all that mattered.

A preliminary cleaning of the room took Tsetseg and me about a week. First we salvaged what we could from the broken furniture pile, then we hauled the rest out to the khuudo and set fire to anything that burned. We cleaned up the broken glass from the window, swept the floor (dozens of times) and chased out every last spider.

The room still looked like hell.

Dressed in rags, we set out to clean every surface in the room. The quality of our cleaning products didn't make the process easy. Everything that we had bought came from the *Kharr Zakh* bazaar in U.B., where quantity and price were the only things that mattered worth a damn. This meant that every bottle of bleach was watered down, every sponge would disintegrate after a few wrings, and broom bristles were guaranteed to shed faster than a balding man who has run out of Propecia.

Using our crappy cleaning products, we attacked the scum and dirt with a fervency that ate at our elbows and stabbed our shoulders with weariness. It was like giving a dirty child a bath... every layer of scum that we washed away would magically reappear as soon as we turned our backs. Each day we would emerge from our cave, sweaty and coated in black residue, crescents of dirt under our fingernails, our backs aching and stooped.

And still the room looked like hell.

When Tsetseg finally decided that the time had come to paint, I was in no mood to drag the process out any further.

"Why don't we just cover up the walls with some posters?" I asked, trying desperately to save some sanity. "What's the big deal about painting the room, anyway?"

Tsetseg visibly recoiled, as if I had thrown a pot of boiling *kaash* at her face.

"Paint", she told me solemnly, "is very important in Mongolia. You do not understand, Eric. They will not take us seriously unless we paint. This is the Mongol way."

"But why?" I insisted.

"It is the Mongol way," was all my counterpart said.

And so we painted.

On Tsetseg's command, we did the walls in a weak sea-green, the color of foam leaking from a sick whale's blow-hole. The floors were slathered in neon orange, the same garish, bright color as a brand-new road cone. The doors and window trim were painted a crude, school-bus yellow.

Circus colors. Disco colors. Puke colors.

The fumes from the cheap Mongol paint were overwhelming. Even with the window and door open, a horrible, invisible haze hovered about us as we worked, forcing us to keep taking rest breaks outside to keep from keeling over from paint inhalation.

"You will see... paint will change everything," Tsetseg promised, as we wheezed for air during one of our frequent breaks.

"I sure hope so," I said, sick to my stomach.

When it was over, my counterpart and I hung a "Wet Paint" sign on the door to ward off trespassers. It proved to have the opposite effect... Tsetseg's plan all along. With no prodding on our part, word gradually got around about the sign in the post office and the American's secret radio project. Whispers began to circulate... people began to pop by for quick peeks... and as they did, a curious thing began to happen.

From out of nowhere, Muunokhoi, the village electrician, volunteered to wire the Ghost Room for cost (provided that he could host his own show whenever we started broadcasting). My neighbor-boss, Khishigtuul, found some broken furniture that the school didn't need, and some of the teachers got their students to spend a day fixing it up and carrying it to the Ghost Room. Old Khuulaan made a beautiful drape for the window, using some spare cloth she'd been saving to make a *del* for her recently deceased husband. Somehow, the word got out that we were looking for volunteers to staff the station, and offers of help started arriving from every Mongol in town who had ever dreamt of hearing their voice on the airwaves.

And it was all thanks to a fresh coat of day-glo orange and a "Wet Paint" sign.

***

But with the new influx of spectators and helpers also came a virus... Boldbaatar, our village governor and radio station benefactor.

At first, Boldbaatar had been content to stay in the background with the others, smiling and gushing about how much progress we'd made, like a tourist gawking at Mount Rushmore. He would only stay a few minutes at a time, lingering just long enough to get a good stare around the room. But as the frequency of the governor's visits increased, so too did their length, and by the time Tsetseg and I began to set up our equipment and perform test runs, his self-invited tours were lasting for hours on end.

Much of our time was spent discussing technical matters. The man had a non-stop series of questions at the ready: *How does the transmitter work? What frequencies are best to broadcast with? How do you position an antenna? Where did you buy your equipment?* And in fact, the depth of the Boldbaatar's queries surprised me. I gradually came to see that his interest went beyond the mere inquisitive... he was trying to learn how to run a radio station. And despite all that he had done for us so far, I found myself growing suspicious. For the life of me, I couldn't quite understand why this man was so interested in the inner workings of our project.

People only show devotion like this for two reasons... love or profit. And somehow, I doubted it was the former.

But Boldbaatar was crafty, and at times like this, he was always able to find a way to remind me that the village government would be paying for the electricity and heat for "our" radio station. In the Gobi, it is wise to never bite the hand that feeds; you might not get another meal for a long time.

And so I tried my best to answer the governor's questions.

If I was "respectful" to Boldbaatar, then Tsetseg was a full-fledged toady. She would immediately cease work as soon as he arrived, cleaning him off a seat and listening with a patient attentiveness to the details of his day. Always deferential, always sycophantic, Tsetseg would titter at the governor's trivial gossip with the aplomb of a single mother at a job interview. Her behavior shouldn't have bothered me as much as it did. But for some reason, the whole thing didn't quite sit right... I had too much respect for my counterpart to see her act this way.

One day when the governor was off on business and we had a moment to ourselves, I broached the subject of Bold-baatar's persistent visits.

"I mean, doesn't it bother you when he just hangs around here all day?" I asked. "Don't you wish sometimes that he would kind of just stay the hell away, so that we could do some work in peace?"

"*Moe*," she chided, wagging her little finger like she was scolding a child. "The government will be paying for the electricity and heat, true? Boldbaatar is trying to help. He wants to make sure our work is OK. He is a good man, and a good governor. I have known him for my whole life. Besides, Mongolians always give respect to our leaders."

"I'm not Mongolian," I reminded her.

"Well... please... pretend you are," she said, giving me a sharp look. "Or we may be sorry."

***

On July 8, a car radio on the west side of Mandalzuud boomed with a secret test broadcast of Bob Marley's "Redemption Song." There it was overheard by a passing grandmother and her teenage son, who immediately went home and told everyone in earshot what they'd heard.

Shortly after, Tsetseg and I had more volunteers than we knew what to do with.

We held our first official radio station meeting after hours in the post office lobby, which Gombo the postman had graciously agreed to seal off and keep open late. The postmaster even produced a dozen folding chairs and arranged them in classroom formation, reserving the only ones with padding for me and Tsetseg.

The meeting had attracted almost three dozen villagers, all eager and altruistic. They were shining, happy souls, each with their own fantastic radio dreams. I recognized most of them from town: delguur owners, honor students, government workers, clinic workers... the usual crowd of achievers and hustlers. But there were many others that I had never seen before, including a couple of herders' wives from the khuudo, and I spent a good half hour making small talk before the meeting began.

To my dismay, that rat Boldbaatar was there as well. He was dressed in his best suit - the one with the tailored stitching - and crashed over to say hello as soon as we made eye contact.

"This is a good thing you have done," he told me in Mongolian, shaking my hand vigorously and speaking with an exaggerated slowness so I could understand. "Very good. Very good."

"Thanks," I replied in Mongolian, feeling like a dog being given a treat. I glanced over at Tsetseg, who was busy explaining the evening's agenda to a cluster of people behind us. "We couldn't have done it without you, Boldbaatar."

He smiled, glancing back at the crowd of his peers. "But you are the one who makes this idea. And the people know this. Yes... yes, they know. Later, I would like to make a speech, if that is OK with you. I would like to thank you and the Peace Corps for all your hard work."

"*Sain bain*," I answered, nodding hesitantly, not thrilled about the idea but not knowing how to refuse.

"You are a good volunteer," Boldbaatar said, letting me walk past. "I am glad that we sent for you."

Not quite sure what he meant, I waved goodbye and went over to get the meeting started. With Tsetseg translating, I explained the whole shebang to the eager throng of Mongols, even though almost all of them had heard the story from Tsetseg many times already. I discussed the technical details, radio station policies, free speech ethics and program development... all the pertinent facts that a good pirate radio volunteer should know.

"What is important," I concluded, "Is that you all realize this is not *my* station, or the *government's* station... it is *your* radio station. It is the *people's* radio station. This is a gift to all of you... and that means you all will be in charge of it. You will *all* be the dargaa. This radio station will be whatever you want it to be... 24-hour music, talk radio, educational programming, or nothing... if that's what you want. That is for all of *you* to decide. But no matter what you choose, there is one rule that is sacred, one rule that must not be disobeyed..."

"Every person in this village – every man, woman and child – has a right to be heard. This is the rule that will keep the radio station fair... if it is broken, the station will no longer be yours. Everyone is allowed to talk. Everyone's voice is important. Everyone is right, and everyone is wrong. Do you understand?"

And I looked out into the crowd of eager faces, and saw that they did.

***

After leading the volunteers through a crash course in how to handle nice things, Tsetseg and I took them upstairs and squeezed them all into the tiny equipment room. We spent the remainder of the evening letting the new volunteers fiddle around with the equipment, as Tsetseg and I went around the room and filled the weekly program schedule as fairly as possible. As we made our rounds, I was surprised by the variety of ideas that our fellow villagers had come up with: music programs, an arts and craft hour, an "ask the doctor" call-in show, a weekly concert series featuring village students...

And then we got to Batbold.

A senior at the village school, Batbold was one of the first curious onlookers to see our original "Wet Paint" sign. The boy had immediately come down and volunteered to host a show, whenever the station was ready to broadcast. He was intelligent but a natural iconoclast - unusual for a Mongolian - and had already been punished many times in school for being "disrespectful."

Batbold told us that he wanted to host a talk show that focused on "Mandalzuud politics." As the high-schooler outlined his idea, Tsetseg glanced at me nervously to see what I thought.

"What will you talk about on your show?" I asked after a moment, warily.

Batbold looked at us with a seriousness that I had never seen from him before. "There are many things that Mandalzuud people are afraid to say," he told us. "And there are many things that are not fair in this village. You said that every person must be heard... well... I think that if there was a radio show that spoke about these things, these people would not feel *alone*. And that is very important."

I studied the boy's eyes and Adam's apple... he was telling the truth.

"Okay," I said, nodding at Tsetseg to pencil his name into the schedule. "We'll try you out with a half-hour show... how about Wednesdays at 1600 hours?"

The boy smiled proudly and nodded. Shaking his hand, I turned away to talk to the next volunteer. But before I could, Tsetseg tapped on my shoulder and spun me around.

"I do not know if this is a good idea," she whispered as soon as the boy was out of earshot. "Batbold is very smart, but he is angry. He will say bad things about many of our leaders... maybe even our teachers... maybe even our governor... maybe even you. And he does not know what his words may do."

I shook my head. "He's right. This is exactly what I was talking about ... everyone is right and everyone is wrong. If Batbold feels that something is wrong in Mandalzuud, he should be allowed to speak. And maybe, just maybe, he might be right about a few of these things."

My counterpart quickly shook her head. "He does not know what his words will do," she repeated, blinking, as she stared past me mysteriously.

I followed her gaze and saw that our governor, Boldbaatar, was standing across the room, looking at us and smiling.

"That makes two of us," I replied quietly.

***

In a short while, Boldbaatar approached me and reminded me that I'd promised to let him address the crowd. "May I talk now?" the governor asked in Mongolian, gesturing grandly towards the waiting crowd of volunteers.

"Sure," I said, taking a step back and waiting for the governor to squeeze past.

As Boldbaatar turned to face the crowd, I moved within whispering distance of Tsetseg and nudged her surreptitiously with my elbow.

"Let me know what he's saying, OK?" I whispered in English, as softly as I could. "I want to know every word."

My counterpart cocked an eyebrow in curiosity, but nodded that she would, and as the governor began his booming speech, Tsetseg gave a word-for-word translation:

"My friends, thank you for being here at the opening of the Mandalzuud radio station. Much has been done here over the past months, and the village government has worked hard to make this project successful. I want to thank all of you for your interest in working for the radio station, and I know that you will all do your jobs well."

The governor gestured grandly in my direction.

"I also want to thank Eric, our brave and compassionate Peace Corps volunteer, who has shown us what it means to be a vol-un-teer. He has come from America, thousands of kilometers across the ocean, to help the Mandalzuud government build a radio station. He does not do this for money. He does this because he cares about Mandalzuud. He cares about the Gobi. He cares about us. And he knows how to serve his government. He keeps the empire strong. That is the meaning of vol-un-teer."

Boldbaatar paused for dramatic effect. His broad forehead was already shiny with perspiration, and he had swelled in size, like a blowfish or a puff lizard. After a long moment, he sharply raised his right hand in the air, like a military man or a courtroom defendant about to swear on a Bible.

"And so, I have personally been inspired to do something good for Mandalzuud as well. I will volunteer to be the radio station's *erkhlegch*."

As he made this declaration, Boldbaatar took a step forward and bowed slightly to the others. Not sure what to make of this, I scanned the faces of the other volunteers – confusion – and then looked over at Tsetseg, who was watching the governor intently without speaking.

"Tsetseg, what did he just say? What's an *erkhlegch*?"

My counterpart took a deep breath before answering.

"It... it means manager," she said, finally. "He says that he will be the radio station's manager."

"He wants to be manager..." I said, letting my question linger in the air like stale milk fumes.

"Manager," she deadpanned, looking at me.

"I thought we agreed to let the volunteers vote on this?" I asked, confused.

Bolormaa shrugged. We both looked over to see our meathead of a governor shaking hands with the other volunteers, as if he had just won a landslide political victory.

"Sometimes things do not work this way in Mongolia," my counterpart said at last. "Do you understand? We have built a nice radio station. It has cost the village nothing. They will all be happy. We should be happy as well. This is a good thing, I think. It does not matter who is erkhlegch."

Tsetseg paused and thought for a moment before continuing. "In America, you say that it is good to use lemons to make lemonade? Perhaps it is best that Boldbaatar is the station manager. Lemons for lemonade. Do you understand?"

And at last, I *did* understand.

We were about to lose control of our radio station.

In another time and place, I might not have cared. But as I watched the governor do his little handshake victory lap around the room, a terrible feeling of sadness washed over me. And as precedes most great or terrible decisions, I acted without thinking.

"Tsetseg," I said, "I need to say something to the others. Will you translate?"

She nodded and waved her hands in the air to get the others' attention. As the crowd of Mongol faces watched me expectantly, I wished I had a podium to stand behind. In compensation, I tried to puff up the best I could.

"I want to thank you all for your hard work today. This has gone better than I'd ever hoped. We will end the training session soon, and let you all get back home. You are all welcome at the station at any time, and you can all consider me a friend. But most of all, I want to thank the people that have made this radio station possible."

I extended my hand dramatically in my nemesis' direction. "Boldbaatar, your governor, has very generously said that the village will pay for the electricity and heat in our radio room. This is very important, and I think that we all need to thank him."

As soon as Tsetseg finished translating my sentence, the room exploded in a flurry of synchronized clapping. Surprised by my public acknowledgement of his promise, Boldbaatar turned to wave at the crowd of volunteers, all the while looking at me out of the corner of his eye with a masked suspicion.

"However," I said when the clapping had died down, "Since you're *all* volunteers – not just our generous governor – I think that it's only fair that we vote to see who will be manager of the radio station."

After Tsetseg translated my words, the crowd erupted in another round of chatter and applause. As they did, my counterpart leaned over and gave me a sour look.

"Why do you make me translate these things?" she whispered fiercely. "Vote? We must let Boldbaatar be the manager. Why do you do this? They will all vote for him, anyway!"

"What's the matter?" I asked, cocking an eyebrow. "I thought that we agreed on voting for a manager a long time ago... so what's the problem?"

Tsetseg shook her head. "Not like this... not like this," she argued, placing her hands on her hips and squaring around to face me. I had never seen my counterpart so agitated, and for a moment it made me pause. But there was too much at stake – and was too much American left in me – for me to back down now.

"We will vote!" I called out to the crowd of volunteers in my best Mongolian, giving my counterpart a resolute look. I began casting around the room for some spare paper and pens.

And that was that.

As he watched me fumble around the radio room and search through drawers for paper, Boldbaatar kept swinging long glances in my direction. I pretended that I didn't see him. As I busied myself collecting all the pens I could find, Boldbaatar went over and spoke to Tsetseg in rapid Mongolian. When he was finished, she walked over to me and touched my wrist.

"Eric... Boldbaatar said that your idea is good, but we do not need to vote. He will *volunteer* to be manager."

"Oh, I bet he will," I said, struggling to keep the sarcasm from my voice. I turned to face the governor, putting on my best smile mask. I looked at him... he looked at me... and in that instant my decision was made.

"Balls on this," I said. "You're not stealing my Good Deed, and that's that."

"*Yuu?*" the governor queried, confused.

"Eric..." Tsetseg cautioned.

"I have something to say," I said, cutting her off. "Will you translate?"

She nodded, apologizing to Boldbaatar with her eyes. "What do you want me to tell him?"

"Not him," I said, gesturing with my chin at the other volunteers. "Them."

As I turned to face the others, I could feel Boldbaatar's eyes drilling into the back of my head. But it didn't bother me... I had passed the point of no return long ago. I cleared my throat loudly, my voice cutting through the noisy room like a lightsaber through margarine. Glancing over at Tsetseg to make sure that she was ready to begin translating, I raised my right hand in the air.

"I know that you've all been here in this tiny room a long time," I said. "So I'll be quick. We will now vote for a station manager."

I looked at Tsetseg. She was staring at me, expressionless to the point of screaming, but she was still translating.

So I continued speaking.

"Write down the name of the person in this room who you think will be the best manager. We will mix them so that the votes are secret, then we'll count them together. Whoever gets the most votes will be our new station manager."

I stopped speaking so that Tsetseg could catch up with her translation. As she did, I looked out at the crowd of Mongols, meeting as many pairs of eyes as I could.

"One more thing," I said after a moment. "I ask that you do NOT vote for me. I'll say that again. Do not vote for me. This is *your* radio station, not mine. And people should not volunteer for a job that they know is meant for somebody else," I said, looking at Boldbaatar emphatically.

"But vote for whoever you want," I said. "After all, it's *your* radio station."

And I passed out the ballots and pens.

***

It was only about seven or eight minutes before the whole thing was done.

Grabbing a plastic shopping bag, I went around the room and collected the ballots. When everyone had given me their slip of paper, I took the bag over to the radio station desk and dumped out its contents. With the entire room watching, I uncrumpled each ballot one at a time and announced the name, recording the result on a sheet of paper.

When it was all over, there were two votes for me.

There were nine votes for Boldbaatar.

But to the surprise of us all – except the fourteen people who had voted for her – the winner was my counterpart... Tsetseg.

When the final vote had been counted, the room was silent for about a minute, before a huge cheer rose from the crowd of volunteers. Even the villagers who had not voted for her were now in full agreement with their peers. They swept up in a wave towards my counterpart, who was standing next to me, dumfounded by the result of the election. For his part, the governor was taking the blow silently, standing impassive in the corner with his arms folded, his face a mask of politeness. It clearly had never occurred to him that this might happen.

Hell, it had never occurred to me.

I pushed my way past the crowd of volunteers to offer my congratulations to Tsetseg, happy that she'd finally gotten the props that she deserved. But when I reached her, I saw that she was staring at me with a shrill horror in her eyes.

"What have you done?" she gasped, speaking in English so that the others couldn't understand.

"What do you mean?" I exclaimed, taken aback. "This is great! This is what we wanted!"

Tsetseg reached out with a trembling hand as if preparing to explain something, but drew back after a cautious moment, as if I was a rabid dog.

"No... no... it is not," she said, her voice suddenly low and subdued. "I understand now. This is really what you believe. Well, let me tell you a truth. The radio station was never *my* idea. It was yours. It was always yours. And you are too selfish to know that Alexei the Russian was right... you do not do these things because you love us. You only want to 'save us'... whatever that means."

I opened my mouth to argue, but she held her hand up for me to remain silent.

"Listen to *me* now... I know that you think the Mongol way is strange. I know that you think we are stupid. You do not care if the sands sing. You do not care if the old ghosts are disturbed, and you do not care about the price your neighbors pay for your ignorance. And now I will have to fix your mistake, American... like I always do."

"What do you mean?" I asked, stung by the way she called me an "American."

But by the time the question had made its way out of my mouth, my counterpart had already turned her back on me. Her face was upturned in a fake smile – a politician's grin – and she walked over to greet the rest of the volunteers and face their torrid congratulations.

And all I could do was walk away, confused.

***

It was three days before Tsetseg would speak to me again.

Even then, our interactions were curt, formal and conducted mainly in Mongolian... my counterpart's own little way of showing me that she was still angry. Our conversations those first few days after the station meeting were solely professional. When I tried to ask her about her family or personal life, Tsetseg would politely find an excuse to beat a hasty retreat: late for a class, needed at the bank, not feeling well... the list went on. There was a conspicuous tenseness to her voice, a strained effort to maintain composure whenever we spoke - like she was holding in a fart, a scream or an insult - venom spiking every word. It was a deliberate attempt on her part to project frustration at me, which I understood. But my ability to read people's facial gestures had grown since arriving in Mongolia, and when I saw my counterpart's eyes, I read a bewildered hurt that echoed my own, a hurt that she refused to vocalize.

"What happened?" I asked her, over and over. "Are you angry because of the election? We can talk about it... there are things we can do if you don't want to be manager. We just need to talk."

But I got nothing. And by the time the opening ceremony for the radio station came around, I wasn't sure if we were even friends, anymore.

***

The opening ceremony was a small affair: me, Tsetseg, Gombo, a handful of volunteers and of course, Boldbaatar. My counterpart and I had planned the ceremony weeks before the messy business of the election, and had mostly meant for it to be a quick photo op so that we had some nice pictures to send back to the USAID folks.

Tsetseg arrived late and with her hair uncombed, and I could tell that she had been up late thinking, drinking, or both. I prepared myself for a lengthy cold shoulder session, but as soon as she saw me, Tsetseg came over to talk... with a smile on her face to boot.

"Well *you* look happier," I remarked, trying to match her smile and not make any sudden movements that would scare her away. "How have you been?"

My counterpart placed a hand on my shoulder.

"I *am* happy," she said in English. "I have been thinking much, the past days. And I want to say that I am sorry."

"Aw, you don't have to..." I began.

Tsetseg cut me off. "Please, I must apologize. I am supposed to be your counterpart. I should not have gotten angry. I said words that are not true, and I am sorry for them. I know that you care about the singing sands, and I know that in your heart, you only want to help Mongolia. You did what was right in *your* mind... and that is the right decision, I think. Sometimes I forget that you were not born here. Sometimes I forget that I was not born in America. Sometimes I forget that there are places in the world that are strange to both of us. And for this, I am sorry. But no matter what I wish, I cannot change the past. What is done is done, as you always say. Lemons for lemonade. And now I will do what I must."

And as Tsetseg said these words, I saw a change come over her countenance, like a burst of sunlight seeping through a murky layer of clouds. It was a calm aura, a blue aura, and it was as palpable in the room as the air that I was breathing. She had come to a conclusion, I realized.

She had accepted her fate.

"We do what we must," Tsetseg said, smiling at me with a sad sincerity. "Thank you for everything you have done, Eric."

"No, Tsetseg... thank you," I replied.

And we both shook hands.

***

Our first day of official broadcasting was scheduled for August 1.

With little left to do at the station until then, I busied myself with my teaching duties, which I had been neglecting ever since starting work on the radio station. One day after lessons as I was cleaning the blackboards, Dashdorj, one of the station's youngest volunteers, popped his head into my classroom to say hello. The ninth-grader offered to help me clean, but I politely turned him down. Dashdorj nodded and turned to leave, then remembering a question he had meant to ask, turned back to face me.

"What time is the meeting tonight?" he asked me.

"What meeting?" I replied, scratching my head and wondering if I'd missed something.

"The radio meeting," Dashdorj replied, shifting his weight from one foot to the other. "What time must we arrive? I have to help my father in the garden, so I might be late."

I stopped cleaning the blackboards. "Radio meeting?" I queried, trying not to let the surprise creep into my voice.

"Ummmmm..." Dashdorj replied slowly, like a party guest who has suddenly realized that he's talking to someone who isn't invited.

I slowly turned to face the boy, hooking my thumbs into my pockets to make myself appear as nonchalant as possible. "There's a radio station meeting happening tonight? Who did you hear this from?"

Dashdorj took a step backwards. "Tsetseg, Bagsh-a."

"Tsetseg told you that there was a radio meeting tonight?" I repeated slowly, to make sure that I wasn't misinterpreting the boy's words.

He nodded uncertainly.

"Are you sure about this? Who will be there... just you?"

He shook his head. "*All* of the radio volunteers must be there, she told us. For the meeting..." he said weakly. "*All* of us."

I paused for a moment in thought. There was no reason to doubt a word the boy had said; my counterpart had told him that there was a radio station meeting, and that's all there was to it. But for the love of it all, I couldn't understand why she would deliberately leave me out of the loop. Things would have been different if we had still been at odds. But as far as I knew, we had gotten over all that. And although I was glad that our new station manager was undertaking initiatives of her own, there was only one question on my mind:

What was she trying to hide from me?

***

That night I crashed the radio station meeting.

I didn't know exactly when to arrive, so as soon as school was out, I waited inconspicuously outside the post office on a stakeout. Around five 'o' clock, I saw a huge group of students make their way to the post office straight from school, and I knew that the meeting was on. Following the students inside, I headed upstairs to the radio station room. When I slowly swung the station door open, I saw that the entire radio station staff was already there... every single villager that had been at our first station meeting. In the general confusion, nobody had noticed my entrance, so I quietly shut the door and crept into the back row of the crowd.

The first thing that I noticed was Boldbaatar's booming voice addressing the crowd.

Boldbaatar... I muttered under my breath. *I should have known!*

Closing my eyes, using every bit of my meager translating ability, I forced myself to focus on what he was saying. Although I couldn't understand every word, I was surprised to discover how much I could, simply by recognizing his speech patterns and vocabulary.

"Friends..." he hollered, "I feel that we have come to a very important decision, today. As your governor, I want to remind you that although our American volunteer is very helpful, he is not always perfect. His ideas are not always perfect. We are Mongolians... remember? We respect our laws... and we respect our leaders. And if our radio station is used to destroy that respect, then maybe we don't need a radio station after all!"

As the governor's voice grew louder, the crowd began to proportionately quiet themselves. I quickly hunched down in the back of the room and remained silent, hoping that nobody would notice me. It was then, through the shifting crescents of space between the shoulders and torsos in front of me, that I saw there was someone standing next to Bold-baatar... a woman... about thirty years old and with a slight pot belly... clad in her nicest dress (the one with no rips or patches)... wearing makeup (which was beginning to run in the stuffy heat of the radio room)... and with posture straight and authoritative, as if she was teaching an English class...

Tsetseg.

My counterpart.

Eventually, Boldbaatar began to wrap his speech up, concluding with a bit about "duty and honor." When the crowd began applauding, I snapped back to attention. The governor took a pompous bow, then diminished as Tsetseg stepped forward to address the group. As the crowd quieted in anticipation, I leaned forward along with them, waiting for our new station manager to address her volunteers.

My counterpart had never been one to shy away from public speaking. It was how she made her living, after all. But to our surprise, when Tsetseg spoke it was with a slow and careful tone, her fragilely enunciated words slicing the air like Ginsu blades.

"Hello," she said, looking out at the eager crowd of faces. "Thank you for coming tonight. As you know, I have been thinking of my life, and my new job as radio station manager. Two nights ago, I finally came to a decision. I am sorry, but starting today, I can no longer be radio station manager... I resign."

The room exploded with a secret energy as the volunteers began to whisper among themselves. Tsetseg cleared her throat loudly and the crowd began to quiet. When she had their attention again she continued. "I am sorry... and I am happy that you all trusted me with your votes and voices. But I have decided. My responsibilities at the school must come first – teaching is a very difficult job – and I do not think that I will have the time to be a good radio station manager. But do not be afraid, there are others in our village who can be. And it is only fair that we ask one of them to now step forward. *Bayarlaa.*"

And my counterpart stepped back.

Before the room could erupt in chatter again, Boldbaatar reclaimed the spotlight. "I want to thank Tsetseg Bagsh for her honesty," the governor said solemnly, clapping his hands together politely until we all followed suit. When we stopped clapping, he held up his hand as if he were swearing on a Bible.

"As your governor, I volunteer to be the new station manager. We will have a clean station with strong leadership, and most importantly, with no *arguments*," he said, spitting out the word with an exaggerated bitterness.

"The village government will handle the news for our wonderful radio station from now on. Any news or politics must be approved by the village government. In fact, *all* political shows are on hold until further notice. Does anyone here disagree?" the new station manager asked, glancing around with a smile that barely concealed his incisors.

Nobody raised their hands. No vote was taken. No voices cried out in protest.

And just like that, my radio station was gone. As Bold-baatar began to lay out the rest of his "new station rules", I silently crept out the back of the room. I left the building and stole away into the dusk. There was no need to hear the rest; I knew what was coming.

To this day, I'm not sure if either Erdenebaatar or Tsetseg ever knew that I was there that night.

Walking home that evening, a silent shame hemorrhaging inside me, I tried to convince myself that losing the station was no big deal. But deep in my heart, I knew that some part of me had died that day. The bastards had won yet again, and once more, the Good People had lost the faith.

And more and more, I doubted that there were even such things as "Good People" in the first place.

$$\sim 18 \sim$$

<u>The Crack Up</u>

It happened a few days after the meeting, when I went to buy some potatoes for dinner.

In small Mongol villages such as Mandalzuud, shopping is a limited activity, done almost entirely at *delguurs*... tiny Mom and Pop general stores. Much like an American 7-11, these tiny convenience stores carry a little bit of everything and a lot of nothing. Delguur owners manage to eke out a meager living by acting as couriers for the village, making bulk-discount supply runs to Ulaanbaatar and then selling the stuff back in Mandalzuud at a small profit. Naturally, such an industry tends to breed some bastards.

Capitalism will do that.

That day, there was only one delguur open, my least favorite of all. It was run by Zolboo and Adya, a shifty-looking husband and wife team who were always doing crappy things to out-of-towners, like refilling plastic bottles with well water and selling them as new. Despite the largesse of money that I was forced to spend there, the pair seemed to have a heavy indifference to me that bordered on polite hostility.

That morning, Zolboo was working alone. He stood behind the counter, disinterestedly watching me as I walked into the delguur. As I entered, he casually lifted a white paper surgical mask to his face that had been hanging around his neck. I didn't take offense. The paper masks had become a trendy fashion item for Mongolian shopkeepers ever since the H1N1 bird flu started making world news.

"I'll take two kilograms of potatoes," I told Zolboo in Mongolian, pointing at the bin behind the counter.

He blinked and loudly yawned behind his mask, then pointed towards the potatoes as if to confirm what I'd said.

I sighed and nodded, then held up two fingers. "*Khoyer kilo avmarr bain...* Two kilos, dude."

"*Khoyer?*" he asked me lazily, more to stall for time than to confirm my order.

I bit my lip. All of the sudden it was becoming really hot in the cramped little delguur, and I was beginning to feel a little crazy. "Please man..." I muttered, "I've had a rough week. *Tomus... khoyer kilos...* goddamn... goddamn it..."

Zolboo grabbed a nearby pocket calculator and looked me over as he decided how much to overcharge, tapping his fingers idly on the counter in a 3/3 time signature. Finally, after about seven measures worth of tapping, he typed in an offer on the calculator and pushed it towards me.

"*I can understand numbers,*" I said in Mongolian, enunciating the words carefully. We had stumbled through this conversation before. "*You don't need the calculator. Speak to me. Oilgojh bain... Oilgojh bain.*"

He gave me a lazy half-smile and nodded, amused by my foolish attempt to speak his language.

"How many tugrugs?" I asked again, trying to get him to engage me in actual conversation. "*Khed ve? Yaamar un-tay ve?*"

Zolboo pointed at the calculator.

"OK, you bastard," I said in English, waving dismissively, dejected and tired. "Fine. Just give me two kilos."

And I held up two fingers.

Victorious, Zolboo slowly sauntered over to the bin and began placing my spuds in a plastic bag. Just then the delguur door swung open, and a dusty herder in a del strolled in, the door swinging shut in his wake like the saloon gate in an old cowboy flick. The desert mongrel came right up beside me at the counter - never looking my way once - and shouted to the shopkeeper that he wanted a bottle of vodka and a kilogram of potatoes. Taking one look at the herder, Zolboo placed the last of my potatoes in the bag and tossed them down on the counter.

I reached into my pocket for some money, but when I looked up, I saw that Zolboo had left me standing there alone at the counter so that he could fetch the herder's order.

"Hey!" I said, waving my money in the air. "Yo!"

But Zolboo kept ignoring me, and began chatting the herder up as he filled a plastic bag with potatoes. I continued to lean on the counter, money in my hand, feeling like I was waiting for a beer at a crowded bar. When Zolboo returned with the herder's potatoes and vodka, he placed them down next to mine on the counter. I tried once again to give

Zolboo my money, but the two were locked in some sort of guttural conversation that I couldn't quite understand, and I continued to be ignored.

As I stood there shiftless at the counter, biting my lip to keep from cursing, I glanced down at the bag of spuds before me. They were small, bulgy things – roughly the size of kiwi fruits - with occasional spots of light green mold and these terrible humpy tumors that coated their surfaces. I had been getting used to the quality of Mongolian delguur food, and if I had been alone, I would have assumed that *all* of the potatoes were lousy and thought nothing of it. But as I glanced at the herder's potatoes sitting there on the counter next to mine, I noticed that his potatoes looked a lot different. They were larger and more uniformly shaped, free of mold, smooth and plump. They were a hell of a lot nicer, without question.

And I realized that Zolboo was trying to push the lousy potatoes off on me.

With that insight, something deep within me snapped... something cancerous... a tumor that had been repressed and slowly growing for months. Like a possessed Baptist speaking in tongues, the venom spewed forth, and I was powerless to stop it... even if I had wanted to. The zit had popped. The boil had burst. The egg had hatched.

And that's all there fucking was to it.

"I know what you're up to!" I shouted in English, wagging my fist at the shocked delguur owner and his patron. "I know what you're both up to! This whole goddamn place is crooked, man! You're giving me the bad potatoes because you think I don't know any better, huh? Well, I know a bad potato when I see it, you bastard! I know a goddamn bad potato when I see it!"

I tore open my bag and grabbed a moldy spud, then slammed it down on the counter. "Gimmie one of the good ones!" I demanded.

Zolboo and the herder stared at me, a dull horror in their eyes. The shopkeeper was clearly lost - shocked into passivity by my sudden insanity - and had no idea what I was talking about. He looked over at the herder, who only shrugged in reply. He looked back to the crazy American, fuming and suddenly dangerous before him, a rattling snake that he didn't know was venomous.

"*Tomuus-oo?*" Zolboo asked timidly after a moment.

"Gimme a good potato, you cocksucker!" I insisted, unaware in my rage that I was still speaking English. "I know that you have them!"

The shopkeeper blinked and said nothing.

"Fine!" I declared crazily. "If you won't give me a good potato, I'll take them all! I'll buy every single one of these filthy spuds! *Avmaar! Avmaar*, you goddamn potato-monger! Swine like you make me sick!"

I dug into my pocket and slammed a 10,000 tugrug bill down on the counter, enough to pay for three times what was in the shopkeeper's bin. The shopkeeper continued to stare at me, bewildered. The herder, lost somewhere between amusement and terror, stood like a statue in the corner of the room.

Neither Mongol said a word.

"Here," I shouted. "Take the money! It's all you under-stand, anyway! All of your potatoes! *Bukh tommuuse! Odoo!*"

Keeping his eyes on me the entire time, Zolboo took an empty rice sack from behind the counter, and slowly crept to the potato bin and began loading potatoes. When the last spud was in the sack, he walked around the counter and held the bag out to me gingerly, as if I was going to stab him at any moment. Slamming my fist down on the counter, I snatched the huge sack of potatoes from his hands and marched out-side without waiting for a response. From my peripheral vision, I saw Zolboo and the shopkeeper follow me out the door like chastised puppies, but so great was my fury that I continued on without missing a step.

I stomped a hundred feet away to a little gully behind the delguur, and thumped the bag down on the ground.

"So you want a Hood Ornament... Well here I am!" I hol-lered, ripping the sack open with my hands. I snatched one of the potatoes and flung it as far as I could into the steppe, watching it land with a thud and a little cloud of dust. The process seemed to encourage some sick impulse in my brain, and I raised my hands to the sky. My balled fists struck viciously at the empty air, like Muhammad Ali having night spasms.

"So this is how it is?" I howled. "I build a radio station for you assholes, and *this* is how you thank me... by giving me the shitty potatoes? This is my goddamn hero's reward? This is the value of a Good Deed? Well you know what I say?" I howled, removing another potato from the bag and letting loose.

"Fuck these potatoes... And fuck all of you, too!"

Another spud launched into the air. Then another. And another. I couldn't stop myself. And as I threw each potato, I kept up my awful ululation: "FUCK THESE POTATOES! FUCK THESE POTATOES! FUCK... THESE... POTATOES!"

I knew that my frenzied cries had begun to attract a crowd, but by then I was so worked up that I didn't care if God itself was watching. "You're not any different from the people in America!" I hollered insanely. "Everyone... everywhere... it's all one, crooked, goddamn mess! Well, fuck that radio station, anyway! And fuck redemption! Who needs it? Who needs any of it?"

"Ffffffffffffffuuuuuuuuuuuuuuuuuuuuuuuucccccccccccccccccccccccccccckkkkkkkkkkkkkkkkkkkkkkkkkkkkkkk Yyyyyyooooooooooooooooooooooooooooooouuuuuuuuuuuuuu-uuuuuuuuuuuuuu!!!"

I took one last potato and wound my arm back as far as I could. Then, putting all my ill will and energy into it, I released, sending the spud sailing through the air like a catapult launching a dove. My momentum spun me around with a violent contraction - a shot putter heaving a cannon-ball stuffed with dynamite - and as the last of the evil energy left my body, I sunk to a knee and sucked in my breath. The potato soared through the air majestically, like a huge, wingless beetle. It landed two hundred feet away, a faraway ooomph accompanying the tiny plume of dust in its wake.

I took a breath.

And just like that, my crack-up was over.

As my fever cleared and the maroon swells faded from my vision, I stood up and looked around in a daze. In addition to the shopkeeper and the herder, there were now another dozen villagers hovering about me at a cautious distance. They were silently watching me, their faces masked in politeness, but their eyes full of a pitying sorrow that made me blush with shame.

What have I done, I suddenly thought in a panic.

The villagers whispered among themselves. A little girl tucked her head into the hem of her mother's del. With the headline - JAPANESE TEACHER MURDERED IN U.B. - flashing through my mind, I got up and walked over to Zolboo, who was standing a dozen feet behind me.

"*Oochlaaray*," I said sheepishly. "You didn't deserve that. I'm sorry."

Zolboo nodded. "*Zuger*," he said, watching me warily.

"No," I told him in English, "It's *not* OK. And there's a good chance that it never will be."

And I turned around and began the walk back to my ger.

<h1 style="text-align:center">~ 19 ~</h1>

Into the Desert and Facing the End

The day after my crack-up, I knew that it was time for an agonizing reappraisal of the entire situation.

Deep in my heart, I knew that my psychotic, potato-throwing episode in the delguur was only the beginning of something yet to come, an opening credo to an utter breakdown of sentient thought. A demon had gotten out - escaped through my throat and fists and soul - and now it was poisoning the people that I'd sworn to serve and enlighten.

I had become a human Chernobyl.

There was something festering inside me, some terrible urge to flee or kill or cry, some feeling that I had buried within myself a long time ago and tried to forget. But the thing had tracked me down to Mongolia, to the middle of the goddamn Gobi, and I could no longer ignore IT... whatever IT was.

Something was waiting for me out there, and I knew that it just might be The End.

Almost two years had passed since I had made my wretched bargain with the suicide hotline worker. I had given it the best try I could; I had fulfilled my end of the deal. Now, only four months from the official end of my Peace Corps career, it had become obvious to me that I'd arrived at some terrible crossroads, and had no clue which road was the correct path to salvation... if there *was* one at all. Now the enemy of the very people that I came to save, rotten and hollow of soul, I was no closer to inner peace than I had been that fateful day – was it so long ago? – when I held that god-damn revolver to my head. I'd walked the thin line as far as I could, and had found the Great Answer to the question that brought me to Mongolia...

What is the value of a Good Deed?

A BAG FULL OF SHITTY POTATOES.

And in my mind, there was only one thing left to do.

*****

I set out for the khuudo a half-hour before sunrise, carrying all of my worldly possessions on my back, bundled up with gear like a Sherpa porter on expedition. My backpack was crammed with two liters of water, a notebook and pen, two apples, a bag of seeds and a bag of peanuts. Tied to this in parcels were all of my teaching materials, radio station notebooks, official Peace Corps correspondence and forty additional pounds of assorted personal belongings and gear.

My guitar I left on the bed, along with a note.

The early morning was cool and cloudy, but I could already see the sun beginning to poke through the purple slog of the predawn, and knew that in a few hours it would be broiling hot out there in the naked steppe. So I set out at a foot-blistering pace, not at all knowing where I was headed, determined to make it so far out in the steppe that there would be absolutely no chance of seeing another human being. I moved quickly through the village, guided only by memory and the faint, bruised-morning glow, whispering feverishly that I was only "going for a walk."

I was NOT cracking up. I was NOT fleeing. I was NOT surrendering.

Only going for a walk. Only going for a walk. Only going for a walk.

But my ability to lie to myself was no longer what it used to be.

As I walked, I thought about ol' John the Baptist wandering out there in his own desert, eating locusts and honey and shitting wherever he pleased. I thought about Neil Armstrong (and those countless other poor fuckers since), wandering around on the Moon, sticking rocks in their pockets and polluting the surface of the Moon with American flags. I thought about the radio station, and Tsetseg, and Boldbaatar, and the Jesus Dentists, and the Dansarans, and the Delgerkhovd Seven, and dead dogs, and stolen money, and mysterious Russians, and frozen water jugs, and dying dinosaurs, and secret graveyards, and desert beetles and singing sands.

I thought about all of these things... and walked... and walked.

***

There are countless ways to die in the Gobi Desert.

Aside from the obvious dangers of dehydration and heat-stroke, a human traversing the Gobi must contend with murderous sandstorms, delirium and exhaustion, a sudden heart attack (for the unhealthier travelers), debilitating accidents and falls, freezing nighttime temperatures, and an entire host of venomous animals and plants. Many a Gobi visitor has fallen asleep somewhere in the desert - perhaps drunk and perhaps not - never to wake up again.

But by far, the most common cause of death in the Gobi Desert is despair. Without the will to live, survival is impossible. Loneliness, fear, mistrust, paranoia... these are all killers with a potency that fangs or landslides cannot hope to match.

And if you're not careful, death can come to you at anytime.

***

Shortly after noon, I came to a small, rock outcropping near the foothills of a tiny steep. On top of the ledge, a dotting of saxaul trees stood rebelliously against the sun, and the winds of the Gobi were damped for a small radius underneath. There was a calm laziness about the place, as if the Gobi had permitted a moment of mercy and allowed a brief flourishing of life.

It's not exactly holy, but it'll do, I thought.

I climbed to the top of the outcropping and sat down in the meager shade of a saxaul tree, resting my back against the cool trunk as I meticulously removed my boots and emptied out the sand and rocks. Then I opened my backpack and drank some of my precious water, sloshing the coolness around in my mouth, while the rest of the desert watched me with a thirsty jealousy. I finished with my meager lunch of apples and peanuts, offering a few cores and crumbs as a tribute to the bugs.

At last, when all seemed right, I took out a Ziplock baggie from my backpack. It was filled with dozens of rectangular, paper packets. I had found the packets buried in a donation bin, deep in the Peace Corps' storage garage in Ulaanbaatar. Some seed company had donated them to the Corps a year or two ago, and they had been laying there ever since, until I had discovered them during Pre Service Training and stuffed all I could find into my pockets.

The time had come for my Secret Weapon... morning glory seeds.

While seemingly innocuous and purely ornamental, the seeds of many varieties of the flowers known as "morning glories" contain a substance called Lysergic Acid Amide, which is but an asshole hair's length away from LSD. The ancient Aztecs, in fact, were known to use morning glory seeds during many rituals and ethereal ceremonies, grinding them into a powder or sometimes extracting the alkaloids via filtration. Mild effects can be felt with as few as 50 seeds, but most people need to eat about two or three hundred to really trip.

I figured that I'd take about five thousand, and that would do the trick.

Tearing open the packets and laying the seeds on a sheet of folded notebook paper, I took a rock from the ground and began to grind them into powder. I didn't stop until every single one of the little, black teardrops was crushed up into particles as fine as hourglass sand. Uncapping the top of my Nalgene water bottle, I carefully poured the seed powder in and shook it up, until the bottle was filled with a thick, husky, seed soup.

I am the oyster, and Fate is the knife, I thought, and drank the whole rotten concoction down in one breath.

When the sloshing in my belly had died down a bit, I gathered myself off the ground and lit a cigarette. Then, calmly and ceremonially, I walked over to my heap of belongings and began piling them in a pyramid on the dusty earth in front of me... my little desert ovoo... my tribute to this Soft Exile gone so terribly wrong.

Onto the heap went two week's worth of socks, boxers and t-shirts, two sets of thermals, two sweaters and pairs of jeans, a surplus U.S. Postal Service winter coat, and a Salvation Army business suit and pants. Onto the heap went my teaching materials, radio station notebooks, and official Peace Corps correspondence. Onto the heap went my Corps-issued, -20 degree rated sleeping bag, and my mosquito net, and my set of poly-plastic snowshoes, and my Mongol-English dictionary. Onto the heap went my official Corps medical kit, with its universe of pills and balms, and non-functioning rape whistle. And then, when all these things had been heaped on the desert floor, I added one last contribution to the pile...

A handmade, Mongol *tsampt* and *khadaad*.

When the sum total of my time in Mongolia was laid before me, I gave the pile one last glance, like a castaway abandoning a sinking raft.

I pulled out my lighter.

"Goodbye to Good Deeds," I told the pile.

And I set it all on fire and walked off into the desert.

***

I knew that it would be an hour or two before the seeds' effects would kick in, so I headed back into the indiscriminate steppe and set out walking aimlessly once again, my shadow an oblong wraith in front, pointing the way to redemption or death.

I might have walked two hours, maybe more, maybe none. It didn't seem to matter. Clouds passed... sky passed... sand passed... rocks passed... I passed. Until eventually, as the sun was reaching its apex in the sky, in an innocuous little valley dotted with dried up little shrubs that science had never bothered to name, as I was looking for somewhere out of the wind to piss, I stumbled onto something that would change my world.

At first it looked like I had discovered a large stupa of some sort, or possibly some sort of shrine... a six-foot long, four-foot thick slab of basalt, half-buried so that it's top protruded from the ground. The edges of the rock slab had been roughly hand-smoothed, and at one end of the concrete there was a simple, pentagon-shaped marker, hand-carved from the Mars-tinted native sandstone of the Dundgobi.

Upon the marker, in traditional Mongol script, the following words were chiseled:

"E. Chimgee... 1962 - 1997."

And I knew that very clearly, I was looking at a grave.

Scanning the horizon, I saw more graves off in the distance and went to investigate. Fifty meters later, I found about three or four dozen more of the same structures, scattered about the steppe at wide intervals. I looked around me at the graves stretching out on the desert horizon, all visible now that I knew what I was looking for, much in the way that a person can suddenly see constellations in the stars or a lizard camouflaged against a rock.

That's when I realized I had stumbled into the secret Mongol cemetery of Mandalzuud.

This was the holy land of the Dundgobi. It had been specifically chosen by the death lama, meticulously marked as a place where the soul could return to the Great Essence. It was the chosen land. It was Providence. It was *Eekh Mongol...* the epitome of the secret Mongolian spirituality.

And I was not supposed to be here.

The briefest flicker of disquiet fluttered through my mind like a passing bee, immediately touching off again as soon as it landed. The promise that I'd made to Tsetseg following Ravjah's death came flooding back, fresh as flashback, as well as her warning about intruding in a Mongol graveyard:

"Do not look for bones that are not yours," my counterpart had cautioned me so long ago. "Do not seek the graveyard."

But I knew that this would be my only chance to say goodbye.

It took me a little over a half hour to find the old man's grave. He was located in a modest plot at the edge of the cemetery, his name and dates adorned on a little bronze plaque that was affixed to the headstone. Although it had been less than six months, the little grave was already starting to erode in the unforgiving desert winds.

I stared down at the headstone for a full minute, not knowing what to say or think. And then, like a dental dam bursting, it all came pouring out.

"Ravjah, you son of a bitch... I'm sorry!" I blubbered, stumbling over the words, regretting their clumsiness even as they left my mouth. "You should have been allowed to die in peace, way before I came here and tried to save a world that didn't need to be saved in the first place. You should have been allowed to take your last shit in solitude. You should have been allowed to die in some great battle, felled by dozens of arrows while defending the khan. You should have been allowed to see one more summer, one more sunset, one more rainfall on the greening steppes of the Mongol khuudo. And I had to come and ruin it all by trying to save you..."

I shook my head sadly. "I've done a lot of bad things in my time, old man, and done very few good things to make up for them. But I came here to let you know one thing... I didn't break your goddamn water cart. And that has to count for something."

As I stood there in the desert seeking penance from a dead man, I could feel chemicals swirling inside me, churning like powder in a snow globe, fueling my mind with a weird energy that bordered on mania. All of the sudden, my stomach began to growl. I could feel the echoes rippling through me, little depth charges going off inside my guts. And without any further warning, I became very aware that the morning glory seeds had jumped me, snuck up on me ninja-fashion... like all the strongest trips always do.

The seeds had taken charge, and there was no turning back.

Like a man possessed, I tilted my head forward. And I threw up, everywhere.

Ancient Mongolian graveyard ghosts shrieked as I emptied my stomach contents in their sacred grove, splattering their hallowed soil with chunks of barely-digested apples and raisins. I emptied my soul and body all over the ground, all over the side of Ravjah's grave, all over the sacrosanct earth around me.

I'm sorry, I whispered to the ghosts between heaves, but I had no way of knowing if they heard me or not. As I began to feel myself blacking out, I thought about how terrible the whole thing was... passing out in a graveyard in the middle of the Gobi... hopelessly lost... no God in sight... no redemption to claim if I died out there... alone... defeated... desperate... with no big secret waiting for me at the end of it all... only puke on my lips and the silence of a dead man.

You didn't break it... I told myself. *You didn't break it ... You didn't break it.*

I tried to throw up again, and nothing came out but dry heaves and morning glory fumes.

You didn't break it.

I fell to all fours, and was surprised at how soft the ground was. I rested my head in the cool dirt.

You didn't break it.

Like a baby crying himself to sleep, I closed my eyes. As I drifted away into the mind that is never remembered, a voice called out to me through the void. It was a voice that I'd never heard before, too impossibly low-pitched to be heard in waking life - even with morning glory ears - booming and stereophonic and somehow glorious. "WE WILL SPEAK WHEN YOU ARISE," it said.

"But who are you?" I asked, as the world began to spin and fade.

"GOD," the voice said.

And darkness took me.

***

When I came to, the first thing I saw was definitely not God.

Instead, I found myself face to face with a Mongolian Death Worm.

All ten feet of the fabled serpent's blood-red segments were corkscrewed in a pile before me, like a monstrous link of sentient sausage. Its tail was slender and pointed, whip-like and piercing, and a series of spiny hairs extended along its stomach and sides... much like a caterpillar from hell. The creature's mouth was a profile view of an uncircumcised penis, its circular, sucker-like orifice lined with pointy teeth capable of completely stripping the flesh from a marmot in ten seconds. And although the worm had no eyes, no ears, I knew that it could sense every move I made.

Demon, I thought, filled with abject horror.

I tried to stand, but my legs and torso were jelly, useless. Like an arachnophobe prostrated before a twenty-foot tarantula, I laid motionless before the cryptozoological terror, waiting to be doused with a burning globule of acid, or electric shocked to cinders, or simply torn asunder by those terrible teeth. I prepared for eggs in my brain, or larvae in my flesh, or some form of terrible interspecies rape that only exists in disreputable science fiction magazines.

I prepared for death or insanity, whichever came first.

Slowly, the Death Worm reared its body up, like a cobra about to strike. It angled its monstrous head to face me, opening its fetid jaws to show me the crimson lining of its ichorous maw. And all of the sudden, just as I'd given up all hope, the same rumbling, subsonic voice that I'd heard before I blacked out appeared in my head anew.

"SO THIS IS IT, HUH?" the voice said. "THIS IS WHAT IT ALL COMES DOWN TO."

I continued to stare at the terrible creature in front of me, watching it in anxious anticipation of the killer strike. But to my surprise, the Death Worm retained the same pose, holding itself at bay for some unfathomable reason.

"... AND ALL BECAUSE YOU LOST YOUR TEMPER AND THREW A FEW POTATOES AROUND?" the voice continued, booming in my head like an echo in a cave.

And it suddenly dawned on me that this goddamn worm was *talking* to me... via telepathy no less. Apparently, insanity had beaten death to the punch.

The Death Worm shifted its weight to one side. "YOU ARE SURPRISED BY MY APPEARANCE?" it queried, its mouth aiming towards me to simulate the effect of speech, but its jaws remaining motionless.

I squinted. "Well, you *are* a monster. Am I dead? Is this Hell? Just what the fuck this is all about?"

The Worm chuckled. "WHAT DO YOU THINK?"

"I think that I'm passed out in the desert, still tripping on those goddamn morning glory seeds, and this is some sort of lucid dream. Right?"

"SOME MIGHT CALL THEM VISIONS," the Worm suggested.

"Nah," I said, suddenly emboldened by the monster's casual attitude. "I think that I'd know if I was having some sort of vision. This is just a dream."

The worm lowered its head segment a tad and slowly wagged it back and forth. "YOU STILL DON'T UNDERSTAND, DO YOU? I KNEW THIS WASN'T GOING TO BE EASY. WE HAD BETTER GET STARTED... WE'VE GOT A LOT TO COVER BEFORE YOU BEGIN YOUR JOURNEY."

The creature paused, deep in thought. I pondered making a break for it, but my legs weren't up to full strength yet, and I knew that the worm would have no trouble chasing me down. So I waited patiently to see what it would say next.

"I AM YOUR GUIDE," the worm said after a minute, "I AM A REPRESENTATION OF YOUR INNER ENERGY, YOUR RE-PRESSED SINCERITY, YOUR SECRET WAY. YOU HAVE BEEN

LOST, LITTLE DREAMER, AND I AM HERE TO SHOW YOU THE WAY BACK HOME."

And then the horrible truth slowly began to dawn on me...

"Wait a minute," I said, "You don't mean to tell me that you're my *spirit animal*, do you?"

The silence that followed said it all.

"My spirit animal is a Mongolian Death Worm," I said dejectedly. "Well that's just fucking great."

"I'LL FORGIVE YOU FOR THAT COMMENT BECAUSE I KNOW THAT YOU ARE IN PAIN," the Death Worm told me.

"Well if you're my spirit animal, where the hell have you been all this time?" I retorted. "I've been going crazy out here in this goddamn desert! Look at me, man! Just look at me!"

The Death Worm paused kindly, waiting for me to stop huffing. "I'VE BEEN HERE... JUST AS THE TRUTH HAS AL-WAYS BEEN."

I whipped around to face the creature, filled with a sudden anger that entirely trumped my earlier fear.

"Yeah? Well, while you were biding your time, waiting for me out here in this fucking graveyard, I was abusing shop-keepers, exploiting children and breaking friendships! I've lost my faith in Americans, I've lost my faith in Mongolians, and I've lost my faith in myself! And now that I'm out here in the goddamn desert - puking in graveyards, setting my belongings on fire, and talking to a goddamn ten-foot worm about the meaning to life - you have the balls to feed me *this* B-list, Hollywood bullshit? But then again, I guess that I shouldn't be surprised, should I? This whole goddamn jour-ney has been a scam... from goddamn L.A. to goddamn U.B.!"

I clenched my fists in frustration.

"And do you know the worst part? I thought this 'saving the world' gig was going to make me feel like I was part of humanity again. I thought that joining the Peace Corps would make me fall back in love with my fellow human beings. But you know what? It didn't. It turns out that it's not just New Jersey. It's not just America. There is no mythical place where the people are pure, and greed is unknown. There is no Shangri-La. There is no heaven. *Everywhere is the same...* it's true... just like Ralph said. Everywhere, people share the same weaknesses, the same hopes, the same apathies, the same insanities. There's no escaping the Sausage McMuffin, is there? Coming here was goddamn pointless, wasn't it? I'm still so full of hatred – the same rotten hatred that poisoned me for twenty years in America - and no matter how long I wear the Foreigner Smile, no matter how many radio stations I build, no matter how much I suffer, I'm not going to get one step closer to redemption out here. Well, you know what I say? Fuck good deeds! I'm tired of the whole, goddamn mess!"

"THAT SOUNDS LIKE YOUR PROBLEM... NOT MONGO-LIA'S," the Death Worm said.

And for the hundredth time since beginning my new life in the Gobi, I was humbled into silence.

'WOULD YOU LIKE TO KNOW THE TRUE ANSWER TO YOUR QUESTION, DREAMER?" the Worm asked after a moment. "DO YOU WANT TO KNOW THE TRUE VALUE OF A GOOD DEED? WELL... LISTEN TO ME NOW."

"YOU HAVE SPENT YOUR LIFE DIVIDING THIS WORLD INTO A FALSE DICHOTOMY OF GOOD AND EVIL, SPARING NOBODY, ESPECIALLY YOURSELF. BUT FOUL DEEDS ARE BORN OF NOBLE PEOPLE EVERY DAY, AS WELL AS MOMENTS OF ENDURING BEAUTY BY THOSE YOU HAVE LABELED EVIL. GOOD? EVIL? THESE CONCEPTS ARE THE COMFORTS OF THE LAZY MORALIST. YOU MUST LAY DOWN THESE IDEAS AS IF THEY WERE HOT STONES. LABELING PEOPLE AS GOOD OR EVIL ALLOWS YOU TO CHOOSE WHO TO HAVE MERCY UPON, JUST AS WE IMAGINE 'GOD' DOES. BUT THIS IS NOT THE PATH OF THE TRUE BRAHMA... THIS IS THE PATH OF THE JESUS DENTIST. WE MUST BE KIND TO ALL WHO SHARE THESE TIMES WITH US... GOOD, EVIL OR HOPELESSLY NEUTRAL. THIS IS THE ONLY POSSIBLE PATH TO SALVATION. WE ARE ALL GOOD PEOPLE. AND WE ARE ALL EVIL - IN OUR OWN WAYS - AS WELL."

"Well if that's true," I muttered, "and good and evil don't matter, how is the world ever supposed to get saved?"

The Death Worm flashed a row of razor-sharp teeth at me.

"SAVED? WHO EVER TOLD YOU THAT THE WORLD NEEDED TO BE SAVED? SAVING THE WORLD IS AN IMPOSSIBLE TASK... ONE THAT COUNTLESS, OTHERWISE GOOD-HEARTED DREAMERS LIKE YOU HAVE WASTED THEIR LIVES PURSUING. THE WORLD IS A PENDULUM SET ON ETERNAL MOTION, AND EVEN THE GREATEST OF YOUR KIND – OR THE MOST EVIL – CAN ONLY HOPE TO TEMPORARILY SWAY IT IN ANY SINGLE DIRECTION. HUMANITY IS A SPECIAL BREED, PERHAPS FATED TO OUTLIVE ITS OWN DECISIONS, AND IT WILL DOOM OR SAVE ITSELF DESPITE ANY ONE

INDIVIDUAL'S BEST EFFORTS. YOU SHOULD NOT TRAFFIC IN CHARITY BECAUSE YOU THINK THAT IT WILL MAKE YOU ONE OF THE 'GOOD PEOPLE.' AND DEFINITELY NOT BECAUSE YOU THINK THAT YOU WILL BE REWARDED IN THE END... OR ENLIGHTENED... OR SAVED."

"Then why do it?" I asked the Great Worm quietly, the breath knocked from me as surely as if I had been kicked in the groin. "Why should we bother doing any good at all?"

"BECAUSE WE ARE FREE..." the Worm said solemnly. "WE DO THESE THINGS BECAUSE WE ARE FREE."

And I looked up at the worm, cowed to my core, knowing that every word was true.

"YOU WANT A SIMPLE REVELATION, DREAMER? YOU WANT A COOKIE-CUTTER MEANING TO LIFE? YOU WANT A MORAL TO THE STORY? WELL, HERE IT IS... STOP TRYING TO EXIST AND FINALLY START EXISTING. QUIT THIS MAD QUEST FOR SALVATION. LEAVE US IN PEACE, AND GO AND FIND YOUR OWN. I SPEAK FOR ALL OF MONGOLIA AND ALL OF CREATION, WHEN I SAY THAT WE RELEASE YOU FROM YOUR GREAT DEBT... WHATEVER YOU IMAGINE IT IS FOR. WE RELEASE YOU, DREAMER... WE RELEASE YOU. YOU ARE FREE."

"But where does that leave me?" I asked, blinking back eye vinegar. "Where do I go from here?"

"AH, DREAMER..." the worm replied, chuckling to itself. "YOU ASK SUCH SMALL QUESTIONS AND EXPECT SUCH BIG ANSWERS. WHERE SHOULD YOU GO FROM HERE? GO *HOME*. YOU REMEMBER WHERE THAT IS, DON'T YOU?"

And I was surprised to find - for maybe the first time - that I did.

The Death Worm rose to its full height, towering high against the setting Gobi sun. "AND SO WE COME TO THE END OF OUR TIME TOGETHER. GO NOW... FORGIVE THE WORLD FOR BEING ITSELF... FORGIVE YOURSELF FOR BEING PART OF IT... AND ABOVE ALL, REMEMBER THE MOST IMPORTANT THING THAT YOU'VE LEARNED HERE... IF YOU CAN."

As it completed this sentence, my spirit animal began to vaporize before my eyes. I shook my head, trying to clear my vision, but the worm continued to blur until it was a fine smoke. Wisps of its essence began wafting away on the wind, returning to the dream world of their birth, returning to legend and myth and sobriety.

"But what's that?" I desperately pleaded, watching my spirit animal disappear before my eyes. "What was I supposed to have learned?"

The creature, by now more shadow than flesh, turned to gaze at me one last time.

"EVERYONE POOPS," it said.

And like that, as simply as it had begun, my time was up.

THE END

~ 20 ~

<u>Epilogue: A Zen Fable</u>

One spring day, the younger monk Gantsogt went on a meditation stroll through the monastery. There he met the Brahma Danzan, who was sitting under a pear tree, watching the sky and smiling.

"What are you doing, Brahma Danzan?" Gantsogt asked.

"I am studying the Dharma," replied Danzan.

Gantsogt looked at the endless blue sky, the green of the grass under Danzan's robes, the gold of the pears on the limb.

"It looks like you're just sitting, Brahma Danzan," said Gantsogt.

"I am," answered Danzan.

"And does the Dharma reveal itself when one sits?" quizzed Gantsogt.

Danzan smiled and leaned his back against the pear tree.

"I am not studying the Dharma," said Danzan, "I am just sitting."

Want more Eric Kiefer stuff? Check out books, music, comics and more at **www.TheKiefer.com**

Also available for sale at retailers such as Amazon, Apple, Barnes and Noble, Smashwords, Bandcamp and more:

The New Zeitgeist: Songs From The Zombie Apocalypse
The New Zeitgeist: A Tale From The Zombie Apocalypse

Spoken Word For The Doomed

Your Seed For The Moon

The Spectre And The Dozer

Life Is Soup. I'm A Fork.